CONSEQUENCE

Or,

WHATEVER BECAME OF CHARLOTTE LUCAS?

By

ELIZABETH NEWARK

NEW ARK PRODUCTIONS

New Ark Productions
148 Newman Street
San Francisco, CA 94110

(415) 648-6834

CONSEQUENCE, Or, Whatever Became of
Charlotte Lucas?

Hugh Thomson's illustrations for *Pride and Prejudice* first
printed in edition published in 1894 by George Allen.

Photograph on back cover by: Allen Nomura

Library of Congress Cataloging-in-Publication Data

Elizabeth Newark
  *Consequence, Or, Whatever Became of
  Charlotte Lucas?*

Library of Congress Catalog Card Number: 97-92274
ISBN 0-9659147-0-4

DEDICATION

This book is dedicated to the
next generation:
my grandchildren,
Phoebe and Hallie Hillemann
and Caiman Dinneen,

And to
LINDA GREENBERG,
who encouraged me
to write it.

Jane Austen readers may find amusement
in identifying those occasional places where
I use Miss Austen's actual words, lifted
unblushingly from PRIDE AND PREJUDICE.

TABLE OF CONTENTS

CHAPTER   PAGE NO.

CONSEQUENCE:

A thing or circumstance that follows as an effect or result from something preceding

Importance in rank and position, social distinction

ILLUSTRATIONS BY

HUGH THOMSON

CHAPTER 1
HUNSFORD PARSONAGE

"...and considering Mr. Collins's character, connections, and situation in life, I am convinced that my chance of happiness with him is as fair as most people can boast on entering the marriage state."

Poor Charlotte! -- it was melancholy to leave her to such society! -- But she had chosen it with her eyes open.

JANE AUSTEN

"Mrs. Collins?

"Mrs. Collins? Mrs. Collins!"

As his voice rose, Mr. Collins struggled to his feet. The letter he was reading slid through his hands and he snatched at it as it fell to the floor. His chair tipped over behind him unnoticed.

It is a truth universally acknowledged that to be heir to an estate is eminently less satisfying than to be in possession of that estate. Mr. William Collins, the Rector of Hunsford, had lived with his expectations throughout a good part of his lifetime. At first, the expectations had been those of his father, and had arisen once it became apparent that Mr. Bennet, the present owner of Longbourn (the estate which was entailed on the older Mr. Collins), and the father of five daughters, was unlikely to be presented with a son by his wife. The senior Mr. Collins, an illiterate and miserly man, had inherited a quarrel with the Bennet branch of the family, which he continued to enjoy, gloating on occasion to his son over the fact that the quarrel would be *finally* resolved on the day the Longbourn estate became his. "An eye for an eye!" snarled the father. "So perish the ungodly!" (Young Mr. Collins had no idea of the cause of the rift and what, if anything, made these quotations appropriate.)

The son, raised in subjection and humility, had as a means of escape chosen the Church as his career, spurred on perhaps by his father's quotations from the Scriptures. Shortly after his ordination, he had by a most fortunate chance been recommended to Lady Catherine de Bourgh at a time when the living of Hunsford, which was in her gift, was vacant. The respect he felt for her high rank, and his veneration (nay, near adoration) of her as his patroness, had filled the shell of his personality left empty by his father's constant belittlement and, as a result of her approbation, he had arrived at a very good opinion of himself, of his authority as a clergyman, and of his right as a rector. He became a curious (to some people insufferable) mixture of pride and obsequiousness, self-importance and humility.

Lady Catherine, for her part, found him exactly to suit her requirements. Veneration (nay, near adoration), she felt to be her due.

On his father's death, when Mr. Collins in his turn became heir to Longbourn, he began to feel a certain curiosity regarding those five cousins he had never seen, the daughters of Mr. Bennet. The father's contempt for the son had taught him in his youth to feel unworthy; the sudden boosting of his self-esteem by his early success in obtaining an excellent living drove those feelings underground; they emerged afresh as a feeling of guilt towards his cousins, mixed with a strong and somewhat prurient interest in them as females (his mother had died shortly after his birth and there had been little exposure to the gentle sex in his life). To assuage this guilt, he sought a reconciliation by letter with Mr. Bennet, telling himself it was his duty as a clergyman, but he had another aim: he had a wife in view. His father's effect on Mr. Collins was such that, even after the father's death, he felt uncomfortable about seeking a reconciliation. He bent over backwards to conciliate both Mr. Bennet and his dead father's shade. He wrote as follows:

> *"The disagreement subsisting between yourself and my late honoured father, always gave me much uneasiness, and since I have had the misfortune to lose him, I have frequently wished to heal the breach; but for some time I was kept back by my own doubts, fearing lest it might seem disrespectful to his memory for me to be on good terms with any one, with whom it had always pleased him to be at variance."*

Thus advancing and retreating in a somewhat crablike fashion, Mr. Collins moved towards his goal. It was Mr. Collins's misfortune that when he visited Longbourn for a reconciliatory visit, of the two cousins he settled on in turn as a likely wife, first Jane, then Elizabeth, Jane was interested in another man, and Elizabeth was of a degree of intelligence and a turn of humor that prevented her taking his offer seriously. Mary Bennet might well have been receptive to his suit but was not given the chance. As it was, Charlotte Lucas, daughter of Sir William Lucas, and Elizabeth Bennet's close friend, knowing herself to have little chance of marriage otherwise, threw herself in his way. Affronted and humiliated by Elizabeth's refusal, Mr. Collins had not questioned his own good fortune in finding Charlotte Lucas so conveniently on his doorstep, so to speak. Like the Hunsford living, she had dropped into his hand; he accepted this gift from the gods and they were married as soon as conveniently possible.

Mr. Collins might well have allowed his resentment toward Elizabeth Bennet to congeal into a new breach with the Bennet family, but this his wife would not permit. And Elizabeth's marriage to Mr. Darcy, wealthy nephew of Lady Catherine, had confirmed to him that it would be best to be on good terms with the Bennets. At the time of the marriage, Mr. Bennet wrote to Mr. Collins as follows:

"Console Lady Catherine as well as you can. But, if I were you, I would stand by the nephew. He has more to give."

Mr. Collins deplored what he had often felt was a certain flippancy in Mr. Bennet's tone but, on due consideration, he felt the advice to be good. He therefore, over the years, continued to bow down to Lady Catherine, while taking comfort in the knowledge that his wife was in regular correspondence with her dear friend, Mrs. Darcy.

When finally, twelve years later, the news reached him that the estate was his, he reacted with what can only be termed high glee.

"Mrs. Collins? Mrs. Collins? Longbourn is mine at last! Mrs. Collins!"

Mr. Collins was in fact so excited by the letter still clutched in his hands that he called out at the top of his voice (a voice trained by regular pontificating in the pulpit), forgetting that he was alone. Realizing this, and feeling somewhat foolish, he made haste to emerge from his study at the front of the house and go in search of his wife. The time was mid-morning, and Mrs. Collins, the former Charlotte Lucas, was hard to find. There were so many places that she might be in the execution of her housewifely duties: in the schoolroom with her older children, in the nursery with the youngest, in the kitchen instructing her cook, or with the poultry maid, inquiring why the hens were not laying, to name only a few.

"Mrs. Collins! Mrs. Collins?"

Mr. Collins continued to call in a loud and nasal voice (he suffered from chronic catarrh). His cheeks were blotched and the tip of his nose was red with excitement; his neck-bands were quite out of control. When he moved, he pranced; when he stood still, he rocked from toe to heel. Dorcas, the parlor maid, came running out of the parlor, her feather duster in hand, and stared at him open-mouthed; Ezekiel, the gardener, poked his shock of white hair through the open front door, bringing with him a pungent smell of manure; and Ellen, the cook, emerged from the kitchen armed with a sticky wooden spoon, ready to repel an invasion of gypsies.

Down the staircase, quiet and composed, came Charlotte Collins, holding her youngest daughter, Eliza, by the hand.

"My dear Mr. Collins," she said. "Whatever can be the matter? Are the pigs in the garden yet again?"

Under her calm gaze, Mr. Collins stopped his fidgeting and tried to straighten his neck-bands. But he could not hold back his news without exploding.

"Mrs. Collins, the most delightful news. Longbourn is ours at last!"

There could be only one explanation.

"Oh, Mr. Collins," said Charlotte. "Has Mr. Bennet died? Dear me, so very sad for Mrs. Bennet and the family. And my poor Elizabeth, how she will be grieved."

Feeling her quiet reproof, Mr. Collins flushed. He endeavored to control his elation and put on a more respectful expression. It was his duty, after all, to mourn for his cousin, however much his instincts urged him to wave his arms and caper.

Thirteen years of marriage had changed them both. Mr. Collins was a pear-shaped man, with a tonsure of pink scalp surrounded by thinning hair. His figure, like his brain, was layered with suet, and his self-esteem had grown with his waistline. Lady Catherine de Bourgh's continued patronage (until her death two years previously) had made him sufficiently prosperous; despite the arrival over the years of five children, the Collinses lived comfortably. But always at the back of his mind and the forefront of his dreams had been his prospects: he was heir to the estate of Longbourn. He would inherit on the death of Mr. Bennet, father of Charlotte's dear friend Elizabeth, married some twelve years to Mr. Darcy of Pemberley, nephew to

6

Lady Catherine. As each year was added to Mr. Bennet's age, so did Mr. Collins's longing increase.

Now Mr. Bennet was dead.

Charlotte Collins, forty, and the mother of five living children, was also fuller in the figure than when she and Elizabeth Bennet sat out together at assemblies. The tight lacing that accompanied the present fashion for full-skirted gowns constricted her waist, and emphasized her matronly bust and hips. Under the muslin cap, the wings of sleek brown hair worn over her ears were lightly touched with silver. The hair was twisted into a large braided knot at the back of her head in a variation of a style becoming fashionable in imitation of the young Queen Victoria, newly come to the throne; Charlotte did not aspire to ringlets. The lines on her face showed that pain and worry had not been strangers; but it was a calm face, and a decided one. Her eyes showed patience, and her lips closed firmly together (as if there were much she did not say); her chin was tucked back with resolution. She had, in the words of the old saying, "made her bed" when she chose to marry Mr. Collins, and she had slept in it for thirteen uphill years. It had not been a bed of roses, but Charlotte was not one to repine. She endured her thorns as best she could, and cultivated her flowers. She governed her small kingdom efficiently and well, and found enjoyment still in many things. Her smile, as she tended her children and went about her housewifely duties, was infrequent but sweet. And her laugh, when she played with her smallest daughter, Eliza, was still young.

And here it is necessary, dear Reader, that I offer you some account of the main events of Charlotte's life since her marriage. Her first child, a large boy, was born a year after her marriage (a *'young olive-branch,'* as Mr. Collins called him, when writing to Mr. Bennet). The boy was christened William Rosings Collins, a combination of what Mr. Collins felt was his due and of homage to Lady Catherine. Even at birth, he was the type of baby that can best be described as 'aggressively legitimate.' In both face and form he resembled his father and, as he grew, the resemblance became still more pronounced. Mr. Collins was noisily proud of him. William became a heavy, non-athletic boy of limited intelligence but good conceit, assertive at the dinner table, timid away from it. His father, naturally, intended him for the Church.

Charlotte's next child, born two years later, was also a boy (Jonathan Lucas Collins), but he came from a different mold. He was slight in stature and not handsome, but he inherited his grandfather Lucas' social nature and his mother's intelligence. Jonathan was a merry soul, loving to his mother and friendly to all the world. (William, of course, was inclined to bully him.) Charlotte was too wise to favor Jonathan, but her eyes smiled when she looked at him.

The following year, Charlotte miscarried.

Two girls came next, Catherine and Anne Maria, two years apart. They were a dull and dutiful duo, with their mother's coloring and their father's brains. Catherine, when in looks, was considered a fine girl; Anne (compared with her sister) was musical. Then came another miscarriage. Charlotte was low in health and spirits for some time, but her fifth living child, another girl, christened Elizabeth Jane, was a changeling. She was born prematurely after a difficult pregnancy and reared with a quiet desperation by Charlotte that withstood her husband's petty importunities and Lady Catherine's recommendation to put the sickly baby out with a good wet-nurse and stop neglecting her parish duties (by which she meant dining at Rosings on command).

Elizabeth Jane, known at home as Little Eliza, grew to delight her mother's heart. From some errant gene (from the Bennet connection, shall we say?), Eliza developed an impish sense of humor. She was small and in looks resembled her mother, gray-eyed and brown-haired, in no way striking. But her love of life illuminated her face; she drew the eye. As soon as she could walk, she tried to dance. Catty and Annie, as her sisters were known, united in trying to suppress her, but in vain. William ignored her, but Jonathan was her protector and her friend.

Two more babies, boys, followed with the passing of time, a year apart. Both died within the year, of the flux. Charlotte had no more children.

Lady Catherine de Bourgh succumbed to a stroke, brought on by excessive self-esteem and a carefully hidden fondness for port wine (taken, of course, medicinally). She spent six months in bed before she died, unable to walk and barely able to talk, imposing her will on her house with constant thumps on the floor of a stout, silver-topped walking stick that had belonged to her late husband. When too frustrated, she was inclined to strike out at the nearest body. At her death, Rosings, her estate, passed under the family trust to her daughter, Anne.

Shortly after her mother's death, Anne married. She was then in her late thirties. Her husband was a former Archdeacon of Marchester (he resigned the post on his marriage), and also a noted organist. He was a man considerably her senior, long known to the de Bourghs. Anne retained the de Bourgh name, and the Venerable Mr. Crabapple acted as prince consort to his pale, delicate, middle-aged lady. Never having been beautiful, disappointed in the failure of her mother's scheme to marry her to her handsome cousin, Mr. Darcy, Anne de Bourgh took to piety and won herself a husband through good works and the Church. His fondness for the architecture of Rosings was also a factor. Mr. Crabapple won Miss de Bourgh by his kind and fatherly demeanor (in such contrast to the well-meaning but smothering tyranny of her mother), and his masterly organ-playing. An instrument was installed at Rosings, and the rooms rang with the strains of Bach and Handel. The housekeeper, Mrs. Jenkinson, formerly Anne de Bourgh's companion (in whose sitting-room long before Elizabeth Bennet had been bidden to practice), kept her door firmly closed.

Rosings thereafter hosted a steady stream of bishops, missionaries, deans, rural deans, rectors, vicars and aspiring curates, together with their wives and offspring. All this was not to Mr. Collins's liking. He felt continually over-watched, his sermons criticized, and his habits weighed in the balance.

But Mr. Bennet was dead at last, and his estate, entailed as it was (to Mrs. Bennet's oft-voiced disgust), passed to Mr. Collins.

Mr. Bennet died quietly of heart failure, one summer evening, alone in the library he loved. When he was found, his fingers were still caught between the pages of a book. While his heir gloated, Mrs. Bennet indulged in strong hysterics, and his daughters mourned.

Mr. Collins was agog to make the move to Longbourn. Now he could escape from the Anglican backbiting and religious in-fighting of his Rosings neighbors, give up his parish duties, and live the life of a country gentleman, for which he felt eminently suited. He began to talk casually of huntin', horse-flesh, and the preservation of pheasants. He considered for at least a week buying a sporting dog, though dogs of all kinds brought on violent attacks of sneezing; he would never have one in the house, though Jonathan and Eliza begged. Charlotte, with a tact born of her affection for Elizabeth Darcy, curbed her husband's impatience to move to Longbourn.

"My dear Mr. Collins, this will not do. Think of Mrs. Bennet's distress if we descend upon her with her husband barely in his grave. You, with your natural kindness and condescension, will be the first to understand her feelings and I know, in your generosity, you will give her time to plan her future life."

Her method of dealing with Mr. Collins was always to ascribe to him the principles and virtues she wished he possessed. By tactics such as this, she could often persuade and guide him to a high standard of public behavior.

How was Mrs. Bennet to be settled? That was the question. Mary and Kitty, who had lived together in Meryton since the death of Kitty's clergyman husband, Theodore Philpott, only two years after their marriage, conferred over their teacups with Mrs. Philips, who was also now a widow and in very comfortable circumstances. Mr. Philips's business affairs had prospered (his specialty was conveyancing) and, when he died, of apoplexy, he was a warm man. Mary Bennet had married her Uncle Philips's senior clerk, a kind but homely man of the name of Shrubsole, and Mr. Shrubsole had taken over much of Mr. Phillips's clientele on his death and was making a comfortable living.

Letters circulated between the Meryton contingent and the sisters whose homes were farther away. Mrs. Bennet had always planned to live with her favorite daughter, Lydia, but this was not to be.

"La, Mama," said Lydia, shrugging a plump and careless shoulder, "That would not be at all the thing. You know my dear Wickham and me are always on the move. You would find it prodigious unpleasant."

Captain Wickham was at that time stationed in Bristol. Mrs. Bennet was reluctant to accept this dictum, but a short visit to Lydia in her latest Bristol lodgings with her six children (one teething), her constantly changing servants and nursery maids, the visits from the bailiff, and her often absent husband, changed her mind. Jane Bingley and Elizabeth Darcy conferred anxiously with Aunt Gardiner on the degree of their duty to their mother, but luckily Mrs. Philips came to her sister's rescue, inviting Mrs. Bennet to share her home in Meryton.

The partnership throve. The two widows (their caps a miracle of black lace) gave whist and loo parties for their numerous acquaintance (a goodly number of widowers and rackety retired army officers among them) and enjoyed themselves hugely. Mrs. Bennet found her new way of life so much to her liking that she almost forgot to resent the Collinses. Mary and Kitty were within easy reach and were frequent visitors, Lydia and Wickham came when no-one else would have them, and Jane and Elizabeth sometimes broke a journey in order to spend a night. The only time Mrs. Bennet became conscious of her nerves was when her grandchildren stayed too long.

Once this move was made, the way was open for Mr. and Mrs. Collins and their family to move to Longbourn. It was a fateful day. Despite a light drizzle, Mr. Collins paced his new possession foot by foot, outdoors and indoors, rejoicing in every shrub and tree in the grounds, and every handsome piece of furniture and elegant drapery in the house. He had, in the past, enjoyed criticizing Mrs. Bennet for her extravagance and love of show; now he felt there was nothing that was not due to his own consequence. The one fly in his ointment was the marked absence of books in the library, which had been established by Mr. Bennet. The books had been his own to do with as he willed; and he had chosen to leave them to his favorite daughter, Elizabeth. They now rounded out the already splendid library at Pemberley. Mr. Collins seldom read and had no interest in literature, but this did not prevent him from feeling disgruntled every time he eyed the empty shelves.

Eliza Collins was four years old when the move to Longbourn was made, and she grew up on terms of friendly intimacy with the families of Mary and such of Charlotte's brothers and sisters, now married, who lived nearby. By the time she was seventeen, she was lively, loving, imaginative and amusing, popular with her cousins. She would never be a beauty, but only strangers commented on her lack of inches and pointed little face. Her father was uncomfortable with her; he preferred his eldest son, recently made Vicar of Highbury and married to a Miss Eugenia Elton, and his elder daughters, who were prim, plump and self-righteous.

But Charlotte rejoiced in her changeling.

CHAPTER 2
LONGBOURN

'But he is, beyond all comparison, the most agreeable man I ever saw ...'

'He is just what a young man ought to be ... sensible, good-humoured, lively, and I never saw such happy manners.'

JANE AUSTEN

It was about this time that Henry Darcy, Elizabeth Darcy's second son, came down from Oxford.

Mr. and Mrs. Darcy had been blessed with three children: a son and heir, Fitzwilliam, known in the family as Fitz, now twenty-five; a second son, Henry de Bourgh Darcy, twenty-two, and a daughter, Juliet Elizabeth, at eighteen one of the recognized beauties in the County of Derbyshire (rivaled only by her cousin, Amabel Bingley). Fitzwilliam was a stalwart young man, in appearance resembling his father, concerned with the management of the estate, with horse breeding, and the excitement of the hunt. Ever since he reached his majority he had been in love with his cousin, Amabel Bingley. The younger son, Henry, was quite different. He was studious, literary, thoughtful, of a slighter build than his brother but strong and active and a skillful wrestler. He was a notable horseman. Juliet, the only girl, loved dancing, parties and admiration, not necessarily in that order.

Elizabeth's marriage had prospered. Secure in Mr. Darcy's love and support, her courage had risen with every attempt by County society to intimidate her. His pride in his "dearest, loveliest Elizabeth" had fortified her against such snobberies and attempted put-downs as came her way, and Mr. Darcy had his own ways of letting such impertinent people know that if they wished to be invited to Pemberley, their behavior to its mistress must be impeccable. Her own intelligence and sense of humor had helped her to make a success of her life as chatelaine of Pemberley. She loved her husband, her family, and the estate, in that order, and blossomed with the years. She had kept her slender figure, to the envy of Jane, who was beautiful still but, after five children, much fuller in body.

To return to the present. Henry Darcy's father presented him with a splendid thoroughbred gelding for his twenty-second birthday, celebrated at Oxford, and Henry chose to make his way home on horseback. Riding across country to reach Pemberley, he decided to break his journey and visit his mother's old home and his Longbourn relations, whom he did not know. He had been only eight when he last stayed there with his grandfather, a crusty old man with an odd sense of humor. Fitz, the high stickler, already at Eton, had thought him eccentric, but young Henry had enjoyed the old man's company, and spent hours with him in the library, Henry on his stomach on the rug, picking his way through a book of myths, maps and monsters, and Mr. Bennet reading Addison, Swift or John Donne. Henry was sorry when his grandfather died.

Since then the question of visiting Longbourn had never arisen. Henry knew the house had been inherited by a Mr. Collins, a distant relative, whose wife was a dear friend of his mother's. Mrs. Collins had visited Pemberley on one occasion, without her husband. But this, he thought was while the Collinses still lived near Cousin Anne at Rosings. Henry vaguely remembered a quiet pleasant woman, dressed in black (had she lost a child? He did not quite remember.), not fashionable, with a manner that expected obedience from the young. But no-one suggested paying a return visit to Cousin Collins.

It was late afternoon when Henry rode up the driveway at Longbourn. The day was fine, the sun shone low in the sky, a blackbird sang in the shrubbery. As he dismounted at the front door, and looked about for a groom, his eye was caught by the slight figure of a girl in a flounced muslin dress, seated on a swing beneath an oak tree. The dress was of white muslin with blue dots, the full skirt spreading gracefully round her. A book and a tabby cat rested on her knees, but her attention was on him.

A groom arrived and took the reins. Henry walked toward the girl, and bowed.

Hallo," she said, looking up at him and smiling. She saw before her a young man, handsome, eager. He was tall and dark, his face thin, his eyes very alive; his mouth, with something sweet in its curve, seemed ready to laugh. He reminded her of one of the miniatures on the wall in her father's study. Yes, of course. It must be. "You have the look of my cousins, the Darcys. I am Eliza Collins."

Her voice was clear and musical. Henry met her eyes and found himself unable to look away. He, the Oxford graduate, the self-possessed son of a notable country estate, stumbled in his response to this slip of a girl with laughing gray eyes. How astonishing, he thought, the very great pleasure a pair of fine eyes in the face of a pretty woman can bestow. Henry, at Oxford in the past year, had begun to write poetry; phrases, luminous phrases, began to stir in his mind.

"I *am* Henry Darcy," he admitted. "But we have never met," he said. "I should surely remember. How can -- how do you know the way we look?"

"My father has copies of the miniatures at Rosings of all Lady Catherine de Bourgh's relatives. They hang in his study."

A green and yellow caterpillar descended on a silken thread from the oak leaves above. It settled on a muslin sleeve and began to crawl earnestly towards a fair and slender neck. Henry knew exactly how his sister, Juliet, would react to such a visitant. He bent forward.

"Forgive me," he said. "An intruder." He carefully picked the caterpillar from Eliza's sleeve; he wished it were a dragon. She looked quickly down and his hand brushed her cheek. At once he was scarlet.

"Oh, just a caterpillar -- an oak moth, I expect. Perhaps we should save it to frighten Catty."

"C-C-Catty?" stammered Henry.

"My sister," said Eliza gravely. "They terrify her."

"They terrify mine, too."

He pulled himself together, and offered her his arm as she pushed the reluctant cat from her knees, slid from the swing, and stood by his side. The cat wound itself round their legs in a figure of eight, mewed pitifully, and bounded suddenly away across the grass.

"Oh, what a beautiful horse," said Eliza, as they walked down the drive, and he felt for a brief moment jealous that her attention should wander so easily from him.

"Do you ride? Should you like to try his paces? He is very gentle."

"Oh yes, please! I should like it of all things. I have a mare, rather old, very quiet. A true lady's horse, my father says. I have always wishes to ride a horse . . . that was not." A small hand clutched his arm, and the gray eyes danced.

"That was not?" Henry was puzzled.

"Not suitable for a lady," said Eliza.

"My saddle!" Henry was dismayed. "I fear that too is not suitable for a lady!"

"I expect we shall manage very well."

The groom was still standing at the horse's head. Henry bent his knee and offered his cupped hand to Eliza as a mounting block. For one giddy moment he felt the pressure of her small foot and the pleasing weight of her form as he tossed her into the saddle. The groom moved away, and Henry walked by Eliza's side, somewhat gingerly holding her in his saddle (not, of course, a side-saddle), as she rode down the drive. He looked up at her and her eyes (those wide-set gray eyes), alight with pleasure, met his. He wished the moment might never end.

Only now, he thought. had he begun to understand the meaning of life.

CHAPTER 3
PEMBERLEY

She now began to comprehend that he was exactly the man, who, in disposition and talents, would most suit her.

"But the wife of Mr. Darcy must have such extraordinary sources of happiness . . ."

JANE AUSTEN

"My dearest Jane," said Elizabeth Darcy to her favorite sister. "Love has broken out like the pox!"

"Lizzie! My dear! Such an expression," said Jane.

Elizabeth blushed. "I blame it all on Fitz. He will use these cant sayings. I am always shocking Mr. Darcy. But in this case I can think of no other way to express it. The romantic attachments of one's children are a constant distraction. Do not, I beg you, be surprised to hear me exclaim 'Oh, my poor nerves -- have you no compassion for my poor nerves?'"

The sisters were sitting in the conservatory at Pemberley, admiring the gardenias blooming under glass and also, since it was late June and the garden door was open to the warm summer breeze, the riot of cream and yellow roses that cascaded over the outside of the conservatory. The scent was dizzying.

"Here is poor Fitz, head-over-heels in love with your beautiful Amabel, and that is charming; we shall all be so happy if it comes to a betrothal. And Juliet has returned from town quite wild about young Churchill -- not the heir, of course, Francis, that would be too much to ask; that would be tame. No, this is Gerard, such a handsome young man, quite delightful in his cavalry uniform. But a younger son and sadly wild -- he has no prospects and, so they say, a mountain of debts! I fear he gambles. Most unsuitable! (His mother is an invalid, and his father does nothing to check him.) And Juliet is just at the stage where she declares that first love is all; she can never love again. She swears she will go straight into a decline, if she cannot marry Mr. Churchill -- or elope -- though with whom I am not sure. And now -- my poor Mr. Darcy is quite without words -- here is my fledgling, Henry -- oh, it seems but a week ago he fell out of an apple tree, stealing pippins, and tore his pantaloons -- well, here he is, barely down from Oxford, not even a full London season at his back, declaring himself in love with Eliza Collins!"

"Eliza Collins?"

"Yes, my dear. Charlotte's youngest daughter, which is pleasant but, oh Jane, also the daughter of Mr. Collins. What is to be done?

"I blame it on the Queen," went on Elizabeth. "A young Queen on the throne, crowned at eighteen, courted and newly married in the full glare of the public's eye within two years. It is too much to bear. All of England is aflutter. Blushes, swoons, heartbreak and decline are all the rage -- though perhaps tight-lacing must bear its share of blame!"

"Have you met Eliza Collins? Is she presentable?" Firmly, Jane Bingley brought her sister back to the subject in hand.

"No, not yet. Henry says she is a sprite, a wren, a moss rose. (Did I mention he sits up at night writing poetry? I wonder if he will make a name as a writer, like that poor young Mr. Keats? But not of course die young! But I digress.) From which I gather that she is small and pale."

"He is not likely to meet her again, if she is not thrown in his way. I doubt if Mr. Collins will give his daughter a London season."

Elizabeth stood up and stretched, and ran her hands down her body over her nipped-in waist to the gathering at her hips. "Oh, Jane, how I detest the corsets that are inflicted on us these days! Remember how free we were as girls? To think fashion should demand such a shape from us!

"Henry insists we invite Eliza to Pemberley," she went on. "Which means of course Charlotte too -- I hope I am always glad to see her -- but then there's Mr. Collins! Mr. Darcy turns quite stiff and silent at the mere mention of his name. I hate to think of him exposed to all the parading and obsequious civility -- and constant chatter -- of Mr. Collins."

"It would perhaps be as well for Henry to see her in his own surroundings. Perhaps she is gauche? Or pert? 'Sprite' can mean so many things. I know," said Jane. "Why don't you give a ball. Juliet will be nineteen in August, will she not? And now Henry is down from Oxford, he should be introduced formally to society. Nothing could be more suitable. A month or so's delay may cool his ardor. And then Henry will see his Eliza among all his friends, and Mr. Collins will be diluted in a river of old acquaintance.''

"My dear Jane!" Elizabeth was impressed. "The very thing! I count on you to help me plan. Now, whom shall we invite? There are a number of young Collinses to be considered. The eldest son, William, is now the vicar of Highbury and is married, I believe, to a Miss Elton, Eugenia Elton. (Charlotte does not like her; she does not say so, but I can read between the lines.)

"And that is yet another reason why it is so important whom one's children marry!" cried Jane. "It must be most trying for poor Charlotte for, as I recall, William is his father's favorite and he must often be asking them to stay at Longbourn."

"Well, at least *we* need not worry about them. And one of the older girls is engaged, if I remember rightly. How many will come?" This was a worrisome point. One Collins was more than enough for Mr. Darcy; a whole litter (as Elizabeth put it to herself) might badly discompose him.

"And I will invite as many eligible young men as I can find. Juliet shall swim in admirers! She too must have a chance to compare. I am anxious for her." Elizabeth went on in a different tone. "She is so willful! We have spoiled her sadly, I'm afraid, our beautiful little girl. Mr. Darcy worries about a possible Collins connection; but when I worry over Juliet I think, not only of Lydia (so reckless), but also of Lady Catherine (so arrogant)! There are questionable attributes on both sides of the family, and what if the two traits combined! When Juliet was a baby, lying in her crib, I was dismayed by the shape of her nose. It seemed to me to bear a definite resemblance to Lady Catherine. Lady Catherine as a baby that is (if she ever were a baby; one's imagination is at a loss)! But she grew out of it -- or into it -- Juliet, I mean.

"But I cannot feel that Gerard Churchill would be a suitable match for her. She needs someone with bottom. Another of her most determined beaux in London was Colin Knightley. He seemed very struck. Both he and Christopher, his twin, are tall and handsome, and very well brought up; there is good blood in that family. Donwell Abbey has considerable history attached to it -- a very fine house, indeed. (And I must confess, dear Jane, that I have always had the tiniest tendre for Mr. Knightley. Mr. Darcy likes him too. He says he's a sensible man, a rare compliment, I assure you.) But Juliet finds Colin somewhat dull. She calls him 'her country squire.' It is only mothers who welcome a dull, respectable suitor. However, he did not make her a declaration, and may well have come to his senses by now, poor young man."

* * *

At ten o'clock that night, Elizabeth joined her husband in his study. He had been out most of the day visiting his tenant-farmers with his steward, and at dinner seemed weary and preoccupied. There had been a rash of rick-burnings in the neighborhood, not Pemberley tenants but close by, and discontent was infectious. The unrest among the working-class was a source of anxiety. But now the house was quiet. Fitz was staying with cousins in Scotland, Juliet and Henry had retired to their rooms, Juliet to try on her latest evening ensemble and pester her maid, Henry to work on his 'Ode to Eliza.'

Mr. Darcy was writing a letter. Elizabeth still enjoyed her moments alone with her husband. She made light conversation for a few minutes, circling round her subject. Mr. Darcy put down his pen.

"Dearest Elizabeth," he said. "Dare I say that you begin to remind me of Caroline Bingley? You are full to the brim with news. If you cannot let me finish my letter, pray tell me what is disturbing you."

"Poor Caroline. So sad she never married," said Elizabeth absently. Caroline Bingley still lived with her sister, Mrs. Hurst, now a widow. Her disposition had not improved. She paid regular visits to the Bingleys and, rather more often, descended on Georgiana Darcy, now married to Lord Charles Baluster.

Henry had arrived home late one night the previous week, and had poured out his world-shattering news at the breakfast table the following morning. Elizabeth had already discussed the problem with her husband.

Now she rose from her chair and took a quick invigorating turn about the room. Coming to rest at his side, she leaned over him, placing one hand on his shoulder and laying her cheek gently against the top of his head. His hair was still thick but silvered, at the sides quite noticeably, and with a sprinkling of white hairs intermingled with the dark beneath her cheek. He was fifty-three.

"It's poor Henry. Jane has had the most splendid idea. We are to give a ball, Mr. Darcy," she said. "To celebrate Juliet's birthday and Henry's entrée into society. Ask all our young people. Then there will be nothing singular in inviting Eliza Collins. Who knows, seen among his friends, Henry may not find her out of the way. And if he still does, well, we will deal with that when we come to it. Charlotte has excellent sense. And Eliza may not care for Henry -- though how she could help it I really do not know," finished Elizabeth, with a touch of indignation in her tone. Fitz, the elder boy and the heir, bore a strong physical resemblance to his father; Henry, the younger son, with a shape of face and color of eye more like her own, strongly resembled his father in disposition; Elizabeth adored them both.

"We are plunged, it seems, into matchmaking," said Mr. Darcy with a tired smile. "It is likely Fitz will marry his cousin, and Amabel is handsome, good-natured and unaffected, very like her mother, yet with something of her father's lively enjoyment of life. They should do very well together. Juliet is young and heedless; she will need guidance, but she may well make a good match. But Henry," he paused. "I admit I cannot like the connection. I should prefer him to make an unexceptionable choice."

Elizabeth kissed his hair. "We shall see. I shall do all I can to turn his thoughts in a different direction. He is over young to think of marriage, after all. Dorothea Brandon is a delightful girl -- or perhaps a visit to France and Italy might distract him, the old Grand Tour?"

Mr. Darcy's hand went quickly up to brush her cheek. "I am sure, Mrs. Darcy, anything you do will be for the best. Shall we retire? I find I am somewhat weary from my long ride today. These rick burnings in the district are worrying. I hope they will not spread to our land."

Elizabeth looked a little conscious. "I would not have you tired for all the world," she said. "By all means, let us go up."

CHAPTER 4
WHOM SHALL WE INVITE?

'I accordingly invited them this morning . . .'

The prospect of the . . . ball was extremely agreeable to every female of the family.

JANE AUSTEN

Juliet Darcy was delighted at the suggestion of a ball for her nineteenth birthday. Her first London season had been a great success; she had received three proposals (though none, it must be admitted, from eligible men), and she was sure -- she was almost certain -- she had lost her heart: Gerard Churchill, delightful in his scarlet regimentals, his tasselled topboots, paraded through her dreams. To be sure, he had not declared himself. He had laughed and teased and flirted, paid her outrageous compliments, escorted her to Richmond Park, and danced her off her feet. But those tender glances as they went down the dance, that gentle pressure of her hand! Such tokens could mean but one thing. All that was needed was the opportunity. Nothing she wanted had so far been denied her; Juliet could not imagine that anything ever would.

Life at Pemberley, after such excitement, was a little flat. There were talks with her mother, and walks with her friends, and pleasant rides with her brother and two young Bingleys. But it was difficult for Juliet to see her cousin Amabel the object of

Fitzwilliam's ardent attentions, while *she* was left to ride with Anthony Bingley, a mere boy (of much her own age), after the heady days in London when *she* was the prime object of attention, and her beaux competed in Rotten Row to ride at her side. Her eyes sparkled at the memory.

Juliet, the third born, favored her mother in looks. Her eyes were her best feature; they were blue and well-opened, set off with long lashes and fine arched brows. Her nose was somewhat high and imperious; her mouth well-shaped but as quick to pout as smile; her complexion glowing. She had her mother's quick charm and lively tongue, though not, perhaps, her intelligence and wit. When happy, she was delightfully pretty, but she was more than a little spoiled and a natural self-importance had been encouraged by the attention shown her by London society. She was always conscious of being the daughter of Pemberley; wherever she was, she must be first. Miss Darcy was known to be rich; she was seen to be beautiful. Impecunious young men flocked round her.

The proposed ball was an answer to her dreams. She worked eagerly with her mother and Aunt Jane, making out lists of those to be invited.

"First of all, Amabel and Anthony," she said, naming two of her Bingley cousins. (Jane Bingley's eldest daughter, and first born, Eleanor Elizabeth, was married to Sir Robert Holywood, and had recently celebrated the arrival of a small daughter. The Holywoods lived in a quiet Knightsbridge square.) "And of course we must invite dear Aunt Georgie and Cousin Lucy, though she is but seventeen." Georgiana Darcy had startled her world by capturing Lord Charles Baluster, third son of the Duke of Broadstairs, a leader in Tory political circles, who remained totally devoted to his quiet lady. Lady Charles carried her position with grace and composure, retiring to her music room when entertaining her husband's political colleagues became too much for her. She retained her deep love and admiration for her brother's wife, finding Elizabeth's wit and irreverence the perfect antidote to the pomposity of politics. She too had three children, a daughter, Lucy, shy and retiring, but with looks that bordered on the beautiful when she was animated, and two much younger boys.

"And then there are the Fitzwilliams," said Jane. Colonel Fitzwilliam had married the striking Lady Moira Douglass, eldest daughter of the Earl of Moray, of Moray Castle, in the Highlands, and a considerable heiress. Elizabeth could still remember the clamor of the massed bagpipes at the wedding. They had several children, two of whom, Catriona and Torquil, both with the flaming auburn hair of their Highland inheritance, were out in London society.

"While we are speaking of relatives, Jane, do you ever wonder about Lydia's brood?" asked Elizabeth. In worrying over Juliet, Elizabeth's thoughts had been invaded by Lydia's unruly presence; it was not conducive to sleep. "Her eldest son, George, is the same age as Fitz, and there must be at least two others over eighteen. I must admit there are times when I wonder how they have grown up, living as they do in the wilds of Ireland."

31

Major Wickham had been killed some five years earlier, while stationed in Dublin, in a drunken brawl following a card game. Lydia Wickham, née Bennet, accompanied by her six children, had shortly afterwards moved in with a local squireen, known as The O'Halloran, with whom it seemed she was already well acquainted. (There had been some unpleasant rumors, much better disregarded, that Mr. O'Halloran had been one of the players at the ill-fated card game.) Lydia wrote at irregular intervals to one or other of her sisters. She seemed happy in her new life -- she never actually described the circumstances of her marriage, nor gave the date of the wedding -- and had produced one more baby, a boy named Dennis Ceiran. She never left Ireland.

"One day we will doubtless find some -- or all -- of them on our doorsteps. If they have Lydia's high-spirits and Wickham's good looks and address, they may be quite out of the ordinary way."

"Indeed yes," said Jane, with a droll look. "Let us hope they stay safely in Ireland until our daughters -- and our sons, for that matter -- are safely married!"

Elizabeth laughed. "Exactly so," she said. She noticed that Juliet was showing interest and hastened to change the subject. "But to return to the eligible," she said "I shall put down the Knightleys. I know Colin is an admirer of yours, Juliet. Both the twins are highly presentable."

"They're dull," said Juliet, shrugging one shoulder disdainfully. "Kit talks about crop rotation and sheep dip. Colin is a little better -- he does at least talk about his horse. And he dances quite well.

But I believe they would both rather ride with their father round the home farm than enjoy the London Season!"

"Dearest Juliet," said her mama. "You cannot expect a Knightley to be sprightly. They have other virtues which you may well come to appreciate in time. Certainly they are both very pleasant to look at."

"And young Emma is still just that. Too young," said Jane, "as are sister Mary's children." Mary Shrubsole's eldest daughter, Beatrice, had died tragically of scarlet fever some five years before at the age of twelve. Her two younger children, Ernest and Myrtle, were now only eleven and twelve. Kitty Philpott, after making her home for years with Mary, had, to everyone's surprise, inherited the Philips' house in Meryton. Mrs. Bennet and Mrs. Philips, the merry widows, had died within a few months of each other and, when Mrs. Philips' will was read, it was found that she had left her house and estate to Kitty, the widow of the next generation.

"But we must have the Churchills," went on Juliet. Her dress that day was a deep coral pink, and it was only natural that the color should be reflected in her cheeks.

"Mrs. Churchill is sadly delicate, but a very sweet and gentle lady. Perhaps she will not come. But Francis and Ger..Gerard," she finished in a hurry. "I am sure they would be happy to be invited."

She was looking out of the window and did not see her mother raise her eyebrows at her Aunt Jane.

"Now the Brandons, I believe we must ask the Brandons," said Jane quickly. "I am so fond of Marianne -- I wish we met more often -- and Dorothea Brandon is growing into quite a beauty, so they say. And if we invite the Brandons, then I think we must ask Nell Ferrars. The family is well connected, although I believe her father -- he is a clergyman -- is not at all well off. Nell does not go much into society. (I have heard it may be necessary for her to take a post as a governess!) But she and her cousin are always together.

"And the young Tilneys, Priscilla and Frederick. And the Wentworths -- Admiral Wentworth married Anne Elliot, you will recall. The young men are called Alexander and Paul. Alexander, the elder, is in the Navy like his father and doing very well, I believe. I must admit to a weakness for the Navy.

"And talking of the Elliots, perhaps the Elliot heir? I believe he is seen everywhere; he has a most polished manner, though his mother is not at all the thing," said Jane.

"He dances very well," murmured Juliet, a smile playing about her mouth. Although Gerard Churchill was her ideal, she could not help being aware of other men, particularly those who seemed to admire her. Colin Knightley followed her constantly with his eyes (was one reminded slightly of a spaniel, or some larger breed? Retriever? Both the twins were tall). But Colin had no conversation, and no one could take the Musgrove boy seriously; Walter William Elliot was a different matter altogether. She had met him at a ball towards the end of the Season.

He was somewhat older than her brother's friends, and not precisely good-looking, with hair that unusual light red, but he had an air of sophistication that intrigued her. When she met his eyes (and he did seem to look at her quite often; nearly every time *she* glanced his way, *his* eyes would be on her), she felt as if she had missed a step -- or a heartbeat. She shivered pleasurably, remembering.

"Fitz says Walter Elliot is a cit," said Elizabeth, frowning at her daughter. "But he certainly has address. And the title is an old one. Did you ever meet Elizabeth Elliot, Jane? -- she married the Earl of Westchester after the death of his first wife, just a year or two ago? She is herself, of course, no longer in the first blush of youth and he -- he must be all of seventy. It was one of the wonders of the year," she went on. "Of the two, the doubtful Lady Elliot -- Sir William's wife -- and the Countess of Westchester, I must confess I prefer the former. Whatever her origins, she is a very pleasant lady, always eager to converse -- while the Countess is so concerned with position that much of her life is taken up in getting in or out of rooms in the correct social order!

"Tom Bertram -- he is now Sir Thomas, of course -- has two daughters, Claudia and Sophia, who are pretty enough, and I believe the Yates girls, their cousins, were part of your set in town, Juliet? Pamela and Angelica, if I have it right. With our neighbors, that should fill the ballroom!

"And now, Jane, we will address the invitation to all members of the Collins family, and we will hope that some of them cannot come.

"The Collinses? Who are the Collinses?" asked Juliet, idly. "Do *I* know them?" This ball was, after all, for *her,* she thought. Her mother and aunt exchanged glances.

"I'm sure you remember, dearest. Mr. Collins inherited Longbourn from your grandpapa. Henry renewed his acquaintance with the family recently on his way home from Oxford. He wishes to return their hospitality by inviting the young people here."

"Are any of them out? Shall I have met them in Town?"

"They are quiet people, Juliet. I doubt very much if any of the girls have been formally introduced to society. But they are your second cousins. I hope you will make them welcome."

"They sound like poor relations," said Juliet, tossing her head. She remembered now, Henry had made a fuss over a girl he had met returning from Oxford. Collins, that was the name. Juliet did not like talking about other girls, and had discouraged him from rhapsodizing. She dismissed the Collinses from her mind.

* * *

On his return to Pemberley from Longbourn, Henry Darcy, Oxford graduate, tried to analyze his feelings, this sudden overwhelming attraction he felt to Eliza Collins, the odd girl who liked cats and caterpillars, looked at him with a prim mouth and laughing eyes, and encouraged him to talk. He had known her just three days. Her father was pompous and dull, her mother calm and pleasant, her sisters unremarkable. Jonathan, Eliza's brother, he liked. The three of them had walked and talked, Henry telling of Oxford, Jonathan of Cambridge, Henry of Keats and Byron and Shelley, and Jonathan of South America and the South Sea Islands, stag beetles and stick insects, while Eliza danced along beside them and turned over logs and rocks, whereupon she and her brother pored over the skittering inhabitants. It was she who listened and, by some apt question and the deep interest she took in all they had to say, set them off again. She was nothing like his sister, or his sister's friends. She was not self-conscious or coy; she made no attempt to attract. Her voice was clear and musical. In the evenings she and Jonathan sometimes sang duets. But it was her face that caught his eye and held his thoughts. She was small and active, and treated him with a casual friendliness that had changed, he thought and hoped, to something very much warmer before he left. He remembered her shy, wondering gaze at him. Eliza. He let her name sing in his mind. Eliza. A poem showed up in his memory, one his tutor had introduced him to, saying he was becoming too serious in his approach to literature. "Try Sir John Suckling, young Darcy," Mr. Lydgate had said. "A little robust humor will be just the thing."

> *Out upon it! I have loved*
> *Three whole days together;*
> *And am like to love three more,*
> *If it prove fair weather.*

> *Had it any been but she,*
> *And that very face,*
> *There had been at least ere this*
> *A dozen dozen in her place.*

That very face, he thought. Eliza.

CHAPTER 5
THE INVITATION

'Who could have imagined that we should receive an invitation . . .'

'... this invitation is particularly gratifying, because it is what I have been hoping to receive; and you may be very certain that I shall avail myself of it as soon as possible.'

JANE AUSTEN

The invitation caused a mixture of elation and dismay in the Collins family.

Mr. Collins, who had adapted well to the prim and proper ways that had come into being with the succession to the throne of the young Queen Victoria (he was a great believer in modesty, virtue and obedience -- for women), saw himself as a figure of considerable rectitude and some importance. His many years as a clergyman at Hunsford had endowed him, he considered, with a decided odor of sanctity; his present position as Master of Longbourn, he felt, had added the glossy sheen of landed gentry to his person. And this collected glory was at last being recognized by Lady Catherine de Bourgh's most aloof relative (he could think of no other reason for the invitation, his first to Pemberley). His triumph in consequence was complete; he was delighted to accept on behalf of them all.

"And I note, Mrs. Collins, the invitation is from Friday to Sunday. An honor indeed. Most obliging, most obliging. Such manners. Such condescension. Of course we shall all go?"

He held the invitation tightly in his hand as if he could not bear to put it down. A sweaty fingermark smudged one edge.

"Indeed, Mr. Collins. This may be a visit of great consequence," said Charlotte. She did not look at Eliza. Under her calm exterior, she felt considable excitement. This was the opening gambit. Pemberley had made the first move.

But Catty and Annie had already accepted an invitation to join the family of Annie's affianced at Sanditon for the month of August. They were beside themselves with mortification.

* * *

When the Collinses' acceptance was received by Elizabeth Darcy, it seemed that only Jonathan would accompany Eliza and her parents to the ball.

"So that is that," said Elizabeth, giving the note to Juliet so that she could complete her lists. "Well, we shall see what we shall see."

But Juliet's mind was full of pink silk -- or should it be white? Or yellow, primrose yellow! She knew how well she looked in yellow, a color trying to many young ladies; few would essay to wear it. Ruffles. Lace. Slippers to match the dress. It did not dawn on her that there was a purpose to the ball other than the celebration of her birthday. (In her way, Juliet was quite as self-absorbed as Mr. Collins.) And Gerard was coming, though Francis could not. All was right with the world.

CHAPTER 6
ARRIVAL AT PEMBERLEY

They live in a handsome style and are rich . . .

*She had never seen a place for which nature
had done more, or where natural beauty had
been so little counteracted by an awkward taste.*

JANE AUSTEN

The ball was to take place on Saturday, August 5th. Carriages began to arrive at midday on the 4th. Only a select few, of course, had been invited to stay from Friday to Sunday at Pemberley; that was for family; and the guest list for dinner on Saturday, immediately preceding the ball, was limited. Those living within comfortable traveling distance would arrive at 9:00 p.m.

The Collinses were among the first to arrive. Charlotte was always punctual. The door was flung wide and the butler and his minions were ushering them inside the main hall when Elizabeth swept down the grand staircase to greet them, with Juliet and Henry close behind. She was surprised to find Charlotte accompanied only by a young man of medium height and a small trim female figure, who must of course be Eliza. Mr. Collins was absent.

"Charlotte!" Elizabeth pressed her cheek against her friend's. "I am so pleased to see you. I hope I see you well. And this is Eliza? And Jonathan?" Her voice ended on a note of inquiry, even as she took in Eliza's small pointed face and large gray eyes, dancing in the shadow of her straw bonnet. Oh dear, she thought. She *is* a charmer.

"Mr. Collins sends his deepest regrets. He is so sorry but a sudden attack of gout has quite incapacitated him. He dare not travel."

[Mr. Collins suffered periodically from gout, brought on by self-indulgence at the table. He was quite proud of it, considering it a sign of good breeding. But he had been bitterly disappointed that an attack should rob him of his first visit to Pemberley. He struggled out of bed on the morning of departure, but the pain in his foot was such that Charlotte firmly bade him return to his couch and remain there. He had also lately complained of a pain in his arm. She looked at his flushed face and noted his shortness of breath, symptoms that had been growing on him with his increase in girth and decrease in exercise. She despatched a servant for Mr. Merryweather, the present Meryton apothecary, and made sure that Mrs. Spong, her housekeeper, fully understood her orders. Mr. Collins was to follow Mr. Merryweather's instructions and was not to rise until Mr. Merryweather gave permission.

"My dear Mr. Collins," said Charlotte. "I deeply regret the necessity of leaving you at such a time, but I fear we might well antagonize Mr. Darcy if none of us responds to his gracious invitation -- the *first* such invitation."

Mr. Collins groaned and assented.

"I leave you in the good hands of Mrs. Spong and Mr. Merryweather.

"I have only one consolation to offer you, Mr. Collins," Charlotte went on. "The new number of Mr. Dickens's periodical has arrived, containing the serial we find so interesting. I have not had time to peruse it. You must tell me all about it when I return."

Mr. Collins approved of Charles Dickens' novels; he had even been known to laugh at Mr. Pickwick's comical adventures. Mr. Dickens perhaps made too much of the undeserving; Mr. Collins found no fault with workhouses and prisons as such but he was prepared to be compassionate at a distance: London was a good way off. The novel at present being serialized was *The Old Curiosity Shop*, and "What will happen to Little Nell?" was on everyone's lips.

Mr. Collins eased himself back on his bank of goosedown pillows. The monogrammed linen cases, freshly changed at Charlotte's direction that morning, were ironed to icy perfection by the laundry maid. He wiggled luxuriously; his gouty foot was protected by a wicker cage under the bedcovers. A jug of lemon-barley water stood within easy reach on the commode at his bedside, together with two fine linen handkerchiefs, and the latest number of the periodical *Master Humphrey's Clock* was just visible poking out from under a copy of *Fordyce's Sermons*. Everything was comfortable and orderly. Mr. Collins regarded his wife's pleasant self-controlled face. He felt a sudden unexpected twinge of melancholy at the thought of her departure, not just because of all he would miss at Pemberley, but because he should be deprived of her calming presence. He himself had made numerous journeys alone over the years, leaving her at home, but not since the loss of her last baby son had she been the one to leave. How would he get on? It was of course, he told himself, a wife's duty to minister to her husband's well-being, but he had to admit that Charlotte was to be priced above rubies in her attention to his comfort. How lucky he had been in his marriage! (Such a mistake as he might have made! One must be grateful to Fate or, he hastily corrected himself, some Heavenly Intervention.) How Charlotte would stare, he thought, if she should know his thoughts, for he was not one to flatter; women were but feeble vessels, easily corrupted by indulgence. Praise should but rarely be bestowed. But -- it came to him now -- his children were dutiful and mannerly, his house was impeccably run, and his dinners well-cooked and well-served -- though without extravagance, always without extravagance. Good management, that was Charlotte's forte. He had a sudden recollection of the home of his childhood, cold, meanly furnished, though his father was not poor, his blankets worn so thin he was forced to add his top coat -- nay, his very jackets - to his bedclothes, the food scanty and poorly prepared by a slatternly underpaid cook-general, the only female presence. Most clearly of all, he remembered his father, unpredictable in his moods, dependable only in his infinite capacity for penny-pinching and petty unkindness. He had feared his father. Despite the warmth of the August morning, he shivered.

"Are you cold, Mr. Collins? Dear me, let me pull up the counterpane," said his wife. "It would never do for you to take a chill." She tucked the counterpane round his chest, then moved to the doorway where Eliza stood waiting.

"Mrs. Collins," he said, impulsively, and held out one hand. But her back was toward him. What was he thinking of? She would think him odd indeed. He let his hand fall to the bed.

"Yes, Mr. Collins?" said Charlotte, turning to face him. "Is there something more you need?"

"Oh -- I trust you will have a safe journey and a pleasant visit."

"Thank you, Mr. Collins." Charlotte looked at her husband with some surprise. His humor was odd, to say the least. It must be the gout, though usually that tended to make him irritable rather than amiable. "Now, say good-bye to your father, Eliza."

"Good-bye, Papa," said Eliza from the doorway. "I am so sorry you are sick."

She could not, although she knew she should, say with honesty she was sorry he would not accompany them. Mr. Collins had a tendency to attract unwelcome notice; he had caused her to blush on so many social occasions. She walked ahead of her mother towards the staircase, but Charlotte hesitated.

Stepping back to the bed, she smoothed an imaginary wrinkle from the sheet, and patted her husband's hand.

"Remember, you are to stay safely in bed. Mrs. Spong will take care of you. Good-bye, Mr. Collins."]

Were Charlotte's eyes twinkling? Her bonnet

shadowed her face. Elizabeth could not tell. She had herself well in hand, despite the sudden elation in her heart. She expressed polite sympathy.

Now she was shaking hands with Jonathan Collins. He was not handsome but his likeness to Charlotte and his sweet-tempered smile impressed her favorably. There was an agreeable sharpness and delicacy in the setting of his eyes, which were gray and well-opened. The footmen were carrying in the luggage. She turned to her housekeeper.

"Mrs. Cleghorn will show you to your rooms. Come down as soon as you are comfortable. Jane is here, and her young people, and everyone is looking forward to making your acquaintance."

The sound of horses' hooves returned her attention to the open front door. A second carriage was sweeping towards them, a crest discernible on the door.

"Why, it is dear Georgiana. How delightful she has arrived in such good time."

The carriage drew to a stop, the steps were let down and a slender lady, in early middle age, descended, followed by a young girl. Elizabeth stepped forward, a smile on her lips, which froze as yet another female form climbed out of the carriage.

"Miss Bingley!" Elizabeth caught a glance from Georgiana Baluster which held a touch of rueful desperation. "Welcome to Pemberley," she said at once, inclining her head with formal courtesy.

Caroline Bingley's affection for her 'dear Georgiana' had continued over the years, punctuated by as many visits to the Balusters's residence as she felt the traffic could bear. She professed extreme affection for Lucy, and did her best to create for herself the role of duenna. Lord Charles, as part of his devotion to his wife, liked her to be at his side as much as possible. "They have trustworthy tutors and governesses, my dear. So please, dearest Georgiana, do not distress yourself so much over the children." Georgiana tried to divide herself as fairly as she could, but a space had been there, and Miss Bingley had inserted herself into it. At a family gathering, she had once heard Mrs. Darcy remark, quite idly, that Henry and quiet little Lucy dealt well together (Lucy was then nine and Henry fifteen). Since that time, Caroline Bingley had appointed herself matchmaker, and continued to do her best to throw Lucy and Henry together. Learning of the proposed Pemberley ball from a letter from Jane to her sisters-in-law, she had descended on Georgiana in just such time as would enable her to accompany the Baluster party to Pemberley.

She now acknowledged Mrs. Darcy's greeting by a gracious bow, turning immediately to Lucy.

"Lucy dear, the sun, the sun! Do go inside, in the shade -- remember your complexion! Nothing so harmful to the skin! Freckles, you know, so vulgar and coarse! And you are looking a little peaked -- a strenuous drive, although dear Lord Charles' carriage is *so* well sprung -- you know you are not strong!"

Henry and Juliet were occupied in greeting the Collinses, but as the newcomers swept into the hall, Miss Bingley seized Henry's arm, neatly cutting him away from Eliza.

"Henry! How good to see you! And how tall you are grown. Your cousin Lucy is a little tired. Do you go and help her."

Georgiana looked annoyed. "Lucy is perfectly well, Caroline. Please do not fuss." Her husband, last out of the carriage, had now joined her and they paused for their introduction to Charlotte.

The housekeeper, Mrs. Cleghorn, patiently waiting in the background, now came forward and led the visitors upstairs. A hasty aside from Mrs. Darcy informed her that the unexpected visitor should be allotted the blue room in the East Wing.

Juliet had fluttered quickly from Eliza Collins to Lucy Baluster. "Dear Lucy, it is an age since we met." Her cheek made brief contact with her cousin's. "Let us all meet in the yellow saloon," she said, "just as quickly as we can."

Jonathan Collins, looking back as he mounted the stairs at the newcomer he had scarcely had time to greet, saw a pensive, heart-shaped face. Her eyes were downcast, showing long lashes in half-moons on her cheeks, as she listened to her cousin's chatter. He paused again as they reached the first landing. The great marble-floored hall beneath him glowed with light from the sunshine pouring through the open doors. A crimson Turkey carpet covered part of the black and white tiles and continued up the staircase. The banisters were picked out with gold paint, and lining the stairway were portraits of imposing people in robes and jewels. The girl mounting the stairs behind him was dressed entirely in white which took on a shimmer of reflected light from sunshine and polished wood and marble and gold paint. Everything was new and exciting, the building grander than any he had previously entered. But it was the girl who held his eye, and at that moment she raised those long dark lashes and looked up at him. He smiled involuntarily, and for a moment her lips too curved upward and her eyes brightened. But just then Miss Bingley spoke, and the girl frowned and looked away. Jonathan took a deep breath.

Mrs. Cleghorn showed Charlotte and Eliza their bedrooms, and then left them together while she escorted Jonathan to his room. Charlotte looked about her with a reminiscent eye; it was many years since she had stayed at Pemberley. She sighed a little. It was a weakness, she knew, but she had always had a liking for consequence. And the splendors of Pemberley were nothing if not consequential. She removed her outer garments, smoothed her hair and joined Eliza.

Eliza was wide-eyed. She took off her bonnet and laid it on a chair, twisting round as she took in her surroundings. There was a four-poster bed with lacy pillows piled high, and a white counterpane. Three little wooden steps enabled one to reach the bed. An armchair, padded with rose-colored velvet, stood by the window; it had polished, curly feet like paws. There was a dresser skirted with lace. Deep rose velvet drapery over white lace curtains festooned the windows, which stood open. The air was warm and the scent of honeysuckle poured into the room.

"Oh mama," said Eliza. "It's like a fairy tale."

She had been silent with wonder ever since the carriage entered the Pemberley grounds, and had watched with shining eyes and parted lips as the house itself came into sight and grew ever closer -- and grander. It was a large, handsome stone building, standing to great advantage on rising ground, and backed by a ridge of high and wooded hills. In front, a stream of some natural importance had been swelled into a lake, but without any artificial appearance. Its banks were neither formal nor falsely adorned. They had descended a hill, crossed a bridge, and finally arrived at the house itself. Every disposition of the ground was good; and Eliza now looked from her window on the whole scene, the lake, the trees -- chestnuts, beeches, oaks, willows bending gracefully over their reflections in the water --and the winding of the valley, with delight. Ducks were swimming on the lake. She was enchanted.

"Yes, my dear; indeed, yes. There is nowhere quite like Pemberley. Now, let me tidy your hair. You need not unpack, Eliza. A maid will do that for you."

"Who was that lady, Mama? The tall thin one all in black, with the acidulated voice?"

"That is Miss Caroline Bingley, sister-in-law to Mrs. Bingley. She has not a happy nature, I'm afraid. At one time, I think she hoped to marry Mr. Darcy -- but I must not gossip. It is all a long time ago.

"Now, if you are ready, my dear, we shall go down."

* * *

The afternoon was not all pleasure for Eliza. She and Jonathan found themselves in a group of young people, comprising not only Henry and her new-found Darcy cousins, Juliet and Fitz, but also Amabel and Anthony Bingley, and the quiet young girl who had arrived so closely on the Collinses' heels, the Hon. Lucy Baluster. They refreshed themselves in the yellow saloon, a very pretty sitting-room, decorated with yellow cushions and hangings, once known as "Miss Georgiana's room," and now Juliet's special domain. And, while they enjoyed a luncheon of fruit and cold meats and little cakes, two more young people arrived, a striking and exuberant pair, Torquil and Catriona Fitzwilliam. The children of Colonel Fitzwilliam, they were both tall, handsome and auburn-haired, confident and talkative and obviously good friends with the Darcys. Exclamations were heard, as the Darcys flocked round them. A stream of family references and "do you remember" dominated the gathering. Jonathan and Eliza found themselves relegated to the edge of the group.

Charlotte Collins sat with Mrs. Darcy and her gentle sister, Mrs. Bingley, in the long saloon overlooking the lake, whose northern aspect rendered it delightful for summer. There also were gathered Lady Charles Baluster and, a little later, Miss Morag Douglass, a cousin of Lady Moira Fitzwilliam, who was acting as companion and chaperone to Catriona Fitzwilliam. Meanwhile, the older menfolk, comprising Mr. Darcy, Mr. Bingley, and Lord Charles Baluster, had made their way to the stables.

Miss Caroline Bingley, to Eliza's dismay, came and went between the two groups, relishing her importance as a guest at Pemberley, but unwilling to relinquish her self-designated post of guardian to Lucy Baluster.

It was Juliet Darcy who set the tone of the afternoon gathering. Her manner was imperious and she seemed to have trouble remembering Eliza's name. Henry greeted Eliza with his old ardor, his eyes lingering on hers as the introductions were made. She smiled back shyly, but as he started to speak, he was interrupted by Juliet, who announced her intention, after they had refreshed themselves, of carrying the girls off to her own room.

"Catriona, I must show you my dress for tomorrow. And you must show me yours. Lucy, what color shall you wear? I hope we shall not all be the same."

Henry tried to divert Eliza to the stables on the excuse of showing her his horse ("Your old friend," he said), but Juliet would have none of it. "Jonathan may go with you, Henry. And Fitz and Torquil," she said with an imperious nod of her head. "*We* will go upstairs. And later I want to show Lucy and Eliza the conservatory." And the young men had obeyed her, though Henry wished to stay with Eliza and Fitz with Amabel. Juliet, thought Eliza, was used to having her own way.

But Henry too had a mind of his own. Even as he accepted his dismissal, he turned to Eliza to say, with a slight bow, "We shall meet this evening, but pray save me tomorrow morning, Miss Eliza. We will ride tomorrow." And then he was gone, leaving Eliza bright-eyed and wistful.

The hours spent discussing dress in Juliet's flouncy bedroom passed slowly. Eliza had one dress made specially for the ball, but her dress for dinner that evening was not new, merely her best. She knew she could not compete with these privileged young women in the matter of apparel. She longed to explore the beauties of Pemberley, both indoors and out. The day was brilliant, and the room grew over warm. Eliza began to make friends with Amabel Bingley, who asked about Longbourn, her mother's old home, and Meryton, and expressed an interest in Eliza's life there. Lucy Baluster said little. Juliet and Catriona kept up an animated chatter on London friends and activities, in which Eliza and Lucy could not join. At last they adjourned to the conservatory.

Here, at least, the glass doors were open to the terrace. Inside, the conservatory was hot and humid; trickles of moisture ran down the windows farthest from the doors. It was a jungly place, thought Eliza. Vines reached to the rafters while below grew exotic flowering plants and shrubs, gardenias and camellias, frangipani and rare orchids. A heavy, heady scent filled the air. Eliza wandered away from the group, moving from plant to plant, smelling the flowers and admiring the brilliance of color and delicacy of individual blooms. Juliet was offering gardenias as accessories for the formal ensembles for the ball.

Eliza found Lucy by her side as she explored the farther reaches of the glassed enclosure.

"Are you interested in flowers?" she asked, attempting to strike up a conversation.

"Our conservatory at Langston Court is one of Mama's great pleasures," said Lucy. "It is not as large as this. Mama teaches me a great deal. And McTavish, our gardener, is my friend. He says I stay still and don't *fratter*, as my brothers do."

"I know more about insects than plants," confessed Eliza. "But the two go together. Some flowers are more attractive to butterflies than others. My brother Jonathan is a naturalist."

"It was he, I think, I met in the hall? There was no time to speak . . ." Lucy remembered a pair of gray eyes and a friendly, admiring glance as she mounted the stairs.

"Yes, he is my dear friend. He is so kind to me," said Eliza. "I missed him very much when he was away at Cambridge. And soon he is taking a post in London with the Royal Society. It is exactly the thing for him, Mama says; she is very pleased. But home will be empty without him."

"How nice for you to have a close friend among your family. I have no sisters, and my brothers are much younger, twelve and nine. Sometimes we play, but they are so boisterous. They rush around and fight and make a great deal of noise."

They had circled the conservatory and drawn near to the rest of the party. Miss Bingley was once again one of the group, and Lucy drew back a little, behind Eliza. But to no avail.

"There you are, Lucy. So hard to find! I was wondering where you could be. But I am always glad to take the trouble. Don't you think it would be better if you rested on your bed? Such a tiring journey!"

"I am very well, thank you, Miss Bingley, not tired at all," said Lucy, looking despairingly at Eliza.

Eliza had just been noticing a perfect spider web, filling a window-pane next to the open door leading out to the terrace. Miss Bingley was quite close to that window. Eliza glanced at her tight-lipped face, thin, corded neck and over-ornamented dress.

"Only see," she said now, pointing out the web to whomever was interested. "One seldom finds a web so perfect. It's as intricate as a lace handkerchief."

Her sleeve brushed the web, and the spider rushed out of hiding. It was fat-bodied, gingerish in color, quite large and very leggy. Miss Bingley stepped hurriedly back behind the other girls, her hand at her heart. Juliet gave a small scream.

"Oh, how dreadful. Do come away. I must tell Cameron to kill it."

"Oh, no, please don't!" cried Eliza. "Spiders do so much good in a conservatory. They help keep down whitefly and mosquitoes and other egg-laying pests, Jonathan says. I think insects are fascinating. Do look, Lucy." She managed to ease Lucy in front of her, closer to the door, pleased to see the other girl seemed quite unafraid.

"Are you interested in natural history?" asked Amabel Bingley, polite but uncomprehending.

"Jonathan teaches me. He is friendly with a young man named Darwin, Charles Darwin. They met at Cambridge. Mr. Darwin sailed as naturalist on the H.M.S. Beagle. They made a scientific survey." Her voice was matter-of-fact, but anyone knowing her well would have caught the mischievous twinkle in her eye. Eliza had long ago learned that it was helpful to know just how people reacted to insects.

"Oh," said Juliet.

"How interesting," said Amabel.

Their eyes met. There seemed nothing else to say in response to such an odd preference. Amabel began to talk about her sister's house in London, where there was a small orangery. Miss Bingley was still at the rear of the group, and Eliza took Lucy's hand and led her out of the door onto the terrace. A cool breeze caressed her flushed face and fluttered her curls, and she sighed with relief.

"Do you know the way to the stables?" she asked her new friend, hurrying her away from the door.

CHAPTER 7
INTERLUDE

*The rain continued the whole evening
without intermission . . .*

*"I wonder who first discovered the efficacy
of poetry in driving away love!"*

JANE AUSTEN

Sunset was not due until after eight o'clock but, by early evening, clouds had gathered and the sky was overcast. A wind got up and tousled the leafy canopy of the great trees in the park. The rooks rose cawing from the rookery and were tossed like ragged black handkerchiefs over the wood. Rain splattered against the window-panes and fizzled on the still-hot terrace paving stones. There was a distant grumble of thunder.

Juliet, who had completed the day in a state of high excitement, plunged at once into despair, lingering on the window-seat and counting out loud the ever increasing raindrops.

"It is only a summer storm," soothed her mother. "Quick to come and quick to go. You will see, my darling. It will soon blow over."

*"Tonight the winds begin to rise
And roar from yonder dripping day:
The last red leaf is whirled away,
The rooks are blown about the skies."*

quoted Henry.

"Oh, Henry, you are always so provoking. Why must you tease with your horrid poetry? You must know I am thinking of our guests tomorrow -- those who come some distance -- from London."

"There was a roaring in the wind all night;
The rain came heavily and fell in floods."

chanted Henry. He had not been happy with Juliet's behavior that afternoon.

Eliza glanced at Juliet's flushed and petulant face, and thought it wise to complete the stanza:

"But now the sun is rising calm and bright;
The birds are singing in the distant woods."

Then she smiled at Henry. "Mr. Wordsworth enjoys his gloomy downpours, but he soon brings out the sun again."

"How well read you young people are," said Elizabeth. "Juliet, don't let Henry depress you with gloomy poetry. Surely you remember some of the happy ones? I am sure dear Miss Underwood (Juliet's governess for many years, Charlotte. A very worthy woman), must have instilled some into you. How about:

My heart leaps up when I behold
A rainbow in the sky."

But Juliet was thinking of Gerard Churchill, rain darkening his fair hair and dripping off his highly-polished boots, gallantly riding through the storm in his scarlet regimentals. Her face stayed as downcast as the weather. Luckily the dinner gong sounded at that moment, and supplied a welcome distraction.

Dinner was served in the small dining room.

The following night, Jonathan whispered to Eliza, it would be served in the grand dining room. There would be fifty guests to dinner. Jonathan had been luckier than his sister. He had renewed his acquaintance with Henry and had made a tour of the house as well as the outbuildings, and accumulated a vast store of interesting information.

The Collinses were seated toward the center of the table. Charlotte pleasantly renewed her acquaintance with Mr. Bingley. Eliza was seated between Torquil Fitzwilliam and Mr. Darcy's steward, Mr. Longacre, neither of whom paid her much attention: Torquil was teasing Juliet about a mutual London acquaintance, Mr. Longacre, a taciturn and weather-beaten man, was interested in his dinner. Eliza employed her time in watching Mr. Darcy, at the head of the table, so handsome and so serious, and Mrs. Darcy, at the foot, so vivacious. She found them both fascinating. Jonathan, seated on the opposite side of the table, next to Catriona Fitzwilliam, was challenged by that lively young lady on the subject of natural history.

"Your sister frightened us all very considerably by introducing us to a spider, Mr. Collins. She mentions worms and snails and slugs with great aplomb. And she tells us that this is a subject in which you are guiding her footsteps. Pray tell me, is it the custom in your family to frighten young ladies?"

Jonathan laughed. Eliza had already mentioned the incident of the spider. He began to discuss, in a light-hearted way, the importance of spiders in the insect world, but also, keeping a solemn face, introduced the large and furry tarantula, the bird-eating spiders of the tropics, and the deadly Black Widow. There were gasps of horror and exclamations from the young ladies. Miss Bingley tried to change the subject ("So disagreeable to the female sex. Quite unsuitable," she said. She was aware that Lucy's eyes were fixed on Jonathan), but other people began to pay attention and, before long, Lord Charles Baluster took Jonathan up. Lord Charles had friends at the Royal Society, it seemed, and he led Jonathan on to talk about his studies at Cambridge, and what he knew about the voyage of the Beagle, and that very odd young man, Mr. Darwin. Science, natural history, paleontology, mycology, ornithology, all were the talk of the day for rational men. The conversation became general. Jonathan, a social being, quiet but not shy, expanded under such encouragement and began to talk, at first amusingly, then more seriously, about the work being done on the natural world. His manner before the older men was good, modest but confident. There was a great burgeoning of interest in all things considered part of the 'natural' world. Collecting was a new enthusiasm. Rocks, fossils, insects, marine animals, birds' eggs -- shore and cliff, forest and hedgerow were pillaged in the interests of science. Much as Mr. Bennet had once collected books, a gentlemanly hobby, educated men now brought home the products of earth rather than the artifacts of man.

When the men were left to their port, Elizabeth

Darcy led the ladies to the Chinese drawing room on the first floor, which opened into the music room. Juliet was eager for an informal dance when the men should join the ladies, and her mother saw no reason to refuse. "Certainly, my dear, she said. "If you can find a willing pianist."

Miss Douglass was quick to volunteer. She was a lively, talkative lady in early middle-age, equally fond of society and her young charges, and always ready to forward their happiness. When the men entered, Juliet whirled her way over to them, her white skirts flaring round her, and seized her cousin Torquil's hand.

"Henry! Henry?" As Henry turned to Eliza, Miss Bingley bustled forward, inserting herself between them. "Your cousin Lucy -- there she is, she's waiting for you, Henry. Lucy? Here's Henry to ask you to dance."

Country dances were thought the most suitable, and Miss Douglass's fingers flew across the keys.

Fitz paired at once with Amabel, Catriona held out her hand to Jonathan and Eliza found herself with Anthony Bingley, with whom she had barely exchanged a word, but she found him a pleasant conversationalist, gentle and friendly.

Miss Bingley seated herself by Charlotte, with much arrangement of skirts and settling of flounces.

"How do you do, Mrs. Collins. It is an age since we last met. Why, it must have been at Netherfield Park!" She gave Charlotte no chance to do more than smile and nod, but continued to speak.

"Look at Henry and dear Lucy," she said complacently. "A charming couple, don't you agree? They have been devoted since childhood. A betrothal would be delightful -- the whole family would be pleased. So suitable, so eminently desirable, don't you think, Mrs. Collins?"

Charlotte watched Lucy and Henry moving sedately down the dance. There seemed no special connection between them. She remembered Elizabeth telling her of Miss Bingley's attempt to cut out Jane Bennet from her brother's affections and marry him off to Georgiana Darcy, all those years ago. Miss Bingley, it seemed, did not change

"You don't feel that there is perhaps too close a relationship, that there might be too much involvement in the family with cousins?"

"Too much, Mrs. Collins? How so?"

"Mrs. Darcy tells me that Fitzwilliam is wild to marry his cousin, Amabel. That seems a certainty. Then Henry and Lucy -- if they have indeed ever thought of such a thing -- again cousins?"

"But the Bingleys and the Balusters are not related!"

"That is hardly the point, Miss Bingley."

"Then what *is* the point, Mrs. Collins?"

"The health of the Darcy family tree, Miss Bingley."

"*Your* family seems to have a strong interest in scientific theory, if that is what it can be called, Mrs. Collins. I find it distasteful in the extreme, and hardly a suitable study for females. *Not* a subject for the dinner table," said Miss Bingley, with an angry titter. "Unseemly, to say the least. The dear Queen must be our model in such things. But perhaps you have a more personal interest at stake? Do not imagine that the family will encourage your ambitions." And she rose and swept away, with an angry rustle of taffeta underskirts and jet bead trimming.

She found a seat close to Elizabeth Darcy and Georgiana Baluster and sat in irritated silence for a few moments, watching as a new dance began. She jerked at the jet beads trimming her sleeves, and played with her bracelets. Catriona Fitzwilliam had claimed Henry, she noticed with approval; Lucy now danced with Fitz Darcy. At least there should be no waltzes that evening, Miss Bingley decided, if she could have her way. No immodest close partnerings. Her hands were never still.

"Caroline," said Georgiana at that moment. "I wish you might not be forever persuading Lucy into thinking herself delicate. She is no such thing. Those of us who have seen her romping with her brothers, playing at cavalry charges or Knights of the Round Table, know that at times she might well be taken for a hoyden! She is only just out and is still somewhat overawed by large gatherings, but that is just a little natural shyness. Her quietness has nothing to do with her health.

"She tells me she finds Eliza Collins a very pleasant companion. They were together some hours this afternoon -- they discovered a litter of puppies in the kennels, and some tabby kittens in the stable-yard. Lucy enjoyed herself very much. I am always pleased when Lucy finds a new friend."

"Do you really think that a desirable friendship, dear Lady Charles? I was dismayed to see Miss Collins make such a dead set at Lucy -- so obviously thinking it would be to her advantage to ingratiate herself. I have no doubt her mama encouraged her to do so. I believe Mrs. Collins was once a friend of yours, Mrs. Darcy? A respectable family, no doubt -- though her father was in trade, as I remember? But Mr. Collins, who is he? A minor clergyman, living on the bounty of Lady Catherine de Bourgh, hanging on the Darcy family coat-tails." Miss Bingley remembered belatedly that Mr. Collins was a distant connection of Mrs. Darcy. She coughed, and touched her lips with her lace handkerchief.

"But Miss Collins hardly shines in the company of our young people," Miss Bingley went on. "Dear Juliet. And Amabel. Quite beautiful! And Catriona so remarkably handsome. And of course dearest Lucy. I must confess I find Eliza Collins sadly plain. Her face is too thin; her complexion has no brilliancy; and her features are not at all handsome. Her nose wants character; there is nothing marked in its lines. Her teeth are tolerable, but not out of the common way; and as for her eyes, they have a sharp, shrewish look, which I do not like at all." Miss Bingley paused at the end of this speech, visited suddenly by a strong sense of *déjà-vu*. Where had she heard those words before? Had she perhaps said them herself on another occasion? She dismissed the idea from her thoughts. *Ridiculous*.

"Indeed?" said Elizabeth coldly. She noticed Henry's sober face. Catriona Fitzwilliam, sparkle as she may, did not seem to be amusing him. Eliza was partnered by her brother. She watched them dancing down the center of the set, Eliza smiling, her feet light, her simple blue dress floating round her. Jonathan too looked happy; he seemed to be teasing his sister. He whispered something in her ear and she laughed up at him. The eyes Miss Bingley had just finished criticizing danced with mischief. Eliza's little pointed face was alive with enjoyment. 'How can anyone call her plain?' Elizabeth thought. The pair were obviously well accustomed to dancing together; they showed no disinclination. Juliet would consider it unfashionable to dance with her brother, thought Elizabeth. She might well be petulant. She watched Eliza and Jonathan with pleasure. The young Collinses were a pleasant pair. The situation was not one to which they were accustomed, but their manners were simple and natural. Despite her initial prejudice, she was coming to like both Jonathan and Eliza.

The final figure was performed and the set broke up, the dancers seeking refreshment. Lemonade was served, and the tea tray was brought in. Someone opened a window, and there was an outcry by Miss Bingley:

"Most unwise! So easy to catch cold. Lucy not strong. Overheating followed by a chill breeze -- just a step to the sickbed! Consumption always possible in a young girl, followed by decline. Dear Mrs. Darcy, this must not be, the young are so heedless."

She was disregarded. Through the open window came a wave of warm moist scented air. The rain had ceased, and those peering out could see that the clouds were parting. The full moon took occasional glances at the earth through the gaps in the clouds.

Juliet's mood improved with a sight of the moon. She stood at the window, playing with the ribbons on her sleeves. "Shall we have some music? Lucy, won't you play for us?"

Lucy glanced in some dismay at her mother, a notable pianist who was also her teacher. But her mother was nodding reassurance. "A simple tune, my dear? Some of the old songs?"

Miss Douglass had long abandoned the piano stool for the tea tray. Lucy sat down and removed her gloves. She played a minor scale or two, then began an old tune that was one of her favorites, "Drink To Me Only With Thine Eyes." Jonathan Collins exchanged a glance with Eliza. They stood up and walked to the piano. As the melody repeated, they began to sing. Jonathan was a tenor, Eliza a soprano; Ben Jonson's immortal words rang out clear and true.

> Drink to me only with thine eyes
> And I will pledge with mine.
> Or leave a kiss but in the cup
> And I'll not look for wine.
> The thirst that from the soul doth rise
> Doth ask a drink divine;
> But might I of Jove's nectar sup,
> I would not change for thine.

Across the room, Henry Darcy, listening, raised his lemonade glass to Eliza. The young people crowded round the piano. Lucy, always shy of singing alone, was encouraged to add her own sweet voice in a descant. Then the others joined in. At the end of the verse Jonathan held up his hand. "Now you must take the melody," he said, smiling at Lucy, and she began the second verse, with the others taking the second part.

Everyone applauded. An encore was enthusiastically requested, and Jonathan and Lucy sang a duet. "Early One Morning" was followed by "The Lass With the Delicate Air." Eliza sang "On Richmond Hill There Stands a Maiden," and everyone joined in the chorus of *"Oh no, John, no John, no John, no!"* Laughter swallowed the tune. Then Miss Bingley interfered, fearing lest Lucy strain her voice, and Lucy was regretfully rising from the piano stool when Jonathan started one last song, à *capella: "I Did But See Her Passing By."* He looked straight at Lucy, who sat down abruptly, in a state of pleasing confusion. She did not play, and Jonathan Collins sang directly to her:

There is a lady, sweet and kind.
Did never face so please my mind.
I did but see her passing by --
And yet I love her till I die.

"Charming," said Elizabeth to Charlotte. "How well he sings. I am impressed with his many abilities."

Miss Bingley snorted. She had the headache. The dancing had been too boisterous, the music too loud. The young Collinses were making a vulgar display of themselves. She longed to be lying on her bed with her nightly dose of laudanum, her great comfort, which brought her sleep and the wild romantic dreams which helped to compensate her for her sadly barren life.

Charlotte Collins watched her son and daughter with a proud heart.

CHAPTER 8
BREAKFAST WITH MR. DARCY

She was shewn into the breakfast-parlour . . .

. . . he was discovered to be proud, to be above his company, and above being pleased; and not all his large estate in Derbyshire could then save him from a most forbidding, disagreeable countenance . . .

JANE AUSTEN

Eliza Collins woke early next morning. She was her mother's daughter, whatever other inheritance she might have, and she had listened to Charlotte and carefully schooled her heart after Henry Darcy had left Longbourn. He was charming, their time together had been delightful, he was everything of which she had dreamed; but three days was not enough for a lasting attachment. So her mother said, and she was right. He must know -- or would soon meet -- so many beautiful, wealthy girls from the first ranks of Society. She would be foolish to count on constancy, though his last words to her had been "This will not end," spoken under his breath as he made his bow.

Eliza was *not* foolish. She tied up her three-day romance with mental ribbons, and put the package away, allowing herself to unwrap just a glimpse now and then in the small hours of the night. But then the invitation had come -- the first such invitation ever from Pemberley. And she had seen her mother's eyes on her as she talked of acceptance, and what they could expect at that Mecca of her father's dreams. Her mother was *so* wise, thought Eliza. But then there was Papa. Sorry though she was at his painful attack of gout, she could not help a moment's thankfulness. The visit promised many obstacles to overcome; one at least was postponed.

She flung her arms wide in the comfort of her bed, which was piled with feather mattresses, so that, lying there in her simple white lawn nightdress with its rows of pin-tucks, she felt like the heroine of a fairy story. She wriggled her toes for sheer joy, then sat up and pulled off her nightcap. Impatient for the day to begin, she slid out of bed and ran barefoot to the window, looking eagerly out. All traces of the storm were gone. The sun was up, and the air was fresh and sweet. Doves cooed on the roof. A green expanse of lawn stretched below her, notable for the complete absence of interruption by daisy or dandelion. Indeed it might be expected that had such an upstart seedling shown its head, it would have wilted directly from feelings of inadequacy. Beneath her window, a cock pheasant paraded across this immaculate lawn, trailing his tail feathers, brave in the knowledge that he was safe from harm for a short while longer; a robin dug for worms. Cream and yellow roses covered the conservatory to her left, the wide borders were filled with lupine and delphinium, lavender, phlox, mignonette and night-scented stocks, and edged with lobelia and candytuft which spilled over onto the grass while, round to the right, she could see two peacocks, seven feet high, clipped out of yew.

Looking farther afield, she saw that the hill, crowned with wood, from which the coach had descended, receiving increased abruptness from the distance, was a beautiful object. Every disposition of the ground was good; and she looked on the whole scene, the river, the trees scattered on its banks, and the winding of the valley, as far as she could trace it, with delight.

And the crowning glory -- she was riding with Henry at eight o'clock.

The previous evening had been difficult at times. Miss Bingley's dislike was obvious, though Eliza did not understand it. She had been allowed only one dance with Henry. She had longed to talk with him (perhaps about poetry? It was so remarkable that they both read Wordsworth), but they had only been able to snatch a few moments' conversation; they were constantly disturbed. Juliet Darcy, too, seemed prepared to resent both her and Jonathan -- or at least ignore them. But dances such as this were few for Eliza. Despite pin pricks, she enjoyed herself. For that matter, there were pin pricks at home. She did not often win her father's approval, and her two sisters both considered it a duty to depress her. Eliza, fortified by the knowledge of her mother's love and with Jonathan's companionship and affection, had learned to deal with pin pricks.

She thought of Jonathan now. As they danced, he had whispered to her of his admiration for Lucy Baluster. He was much taken with her shy charm and big dark eyes. Just for a moment, Eliza had been a little hurt; this was the first time she had seen

Jonathan in the throes of admiration for another girl -- she had never had to share his affection. But almost at once she was pleased, and proud that he should confide in her. And she liked Lucy. The time she had spent with her, after they left the conservatory, had been happy. They had not talked a great deal, but Lucy, delighted to display the wonders of Pemberley, where she had often stayed since childhood, to a new and undemanding friend who seemed ready to enjoy everything that came her way, had revealed more than she thought about herself. Lucy had not yet acquired the veneer of sophistication that her cousin Juliet displayed. Her idea of Pemberley's glories included a tree where a wren nested each spring ("such a dear little nest"); the rap, rap, rap of a woodpecker; deer in the Park, new foals in a meadow beyond the stables; hound puppies tumbling about their placid mother at the kennels. After the stuffy confinement of the afternoon, with its interminable conversations about dress, parties and beaux, the change had been a joy to Eliza.

But Miss Bingley, in throwing Henry and Lucy together so determinedly, had succeeded in keeping both Eliza and Jonathan at a distance. Jonathan had managed to dance with Lucy twice, however, though they had had little chance for conversation.

Eliza did not want to disturb her mother, and was not quite sure where Jonathan was sleeping. She dressed in her riding habit, her brown curls brushed and tied simply back with a blue ribbon. Then, her hat and her gloves in her hand, she left her room and went quietly down the grand staircase, sliding her hand pleasurably down the highly polished wood, hoping to find a side door into the grounds. All was quiet as she descended, though she knew enough to imagine the ordered chaos in the kitchen and butler's pantry, as the staff prepared for the ball. But as she reached the hall, a door opened and a man came out, tall and upright, grave of face, not young but very handsome, his dark hair streaked with silver.

It was Mr. Darcy. Eliza turned quite cold. Her mother had talked of Mr. Darcy, of his high position in Society, his pride and aloofness. Mr. Collins, said Mrs. Collins, had never found favor with Mr. Darcy. And on his marriage to Elizabeth Bennet and the consequent quarrel with Lady Catherine de Bourgh, Mr. Collins, as Lady Catherine's protégé, had been dyed with her colors. It had been many a year before the Darcys visited Rosings. And, Charlotte went on to say, while she herself had been invited to Pemberley after the death of her last baby son ("Oh, so many years ago, my dear"), when her health had been a cause for anxiety, Mr. Collins had not. Eliza knew why her mother had made a point of telling her this history; it would be from Mr. Darcy that strong opposition might come to Eliza's possible connection with Henry Darcy.

Eliza had been introduced to Mr. Darcy the previous evening at dinner, but she did not expect him to remember her. There had been a number of guests, all of far more importance than the Collinses. They had exchanged no words. But she had looked at him when she could -- noting his likeness to Henry, not the close physical likeness of Fitz, the elder son, who matched his father in height and breadth and feature (though Henry too was tall); this was a likeness of expression, of a certain thoughtful glance, a tone of voice, a courteous inclination of the head. Mr. Darcy's bearing showed him to be proud; but she did not find him repulsive. She thought she might like him -- because of that very similarity to Henry.

Now she dropped a curtsey. "Mr. Darcy," she said, in a small voice.

He bowed to her gravely. "An early riser, like myself," he said. "May I conduct you to the breakfast parlor?"

Servants came on silent feet through a baize door at the back of the hall. Another door was opened. Eliza found herself in a pleasant room, the table laid and, from the sideboard, sufficient enticing smells to remind her that she had been too excited to eat much dinner the previous night.

She allowed herself to be seated, and chose to try the kedgeree, because she had never tasted it. It was very good, and she ate delicately, while her host was handed a large helping of deviled kidneys. She sat in silence, gradually relaxing, not uncomfortable, aware of everything about her, the grandfather clock, with its slow, mellow tick, the pleasing proportions of the room, the trim parlormaids in their morning pink-striped cotton, with lace on their crisp aprons and caps; the silver coffee service, the dish of fruit (such rosy peaches!) in the center of the table; a dog barking outside, a deep bell-like sound, not far away. But most of all she was aware of the quiet, aloof man sitting opposite her.

Mr. Darcy, who had been somewhat taken aback to find a strange young visitor invading his breakfast privacy, always most carefully preserved, became more and more pleased as he was allowed to eat in silence. Unobtrusively, he took stock of her. This young lady sitting so upright opposite him did not seem awkward or embarrassed; her quiet was a part of herself. He began to approve of her. Noticing the direction of her gaze, he signed to the butler to bring the silver fruit bowl closer, and invited her to partake. She reached for a peach but just then an ant appeared, plainly visible, scurrying over the rough velvet skin of the fruit. Lines appeared on Mr. Latchett's face, running from nose to mouth, as he compressed his lips, and he "tsk'd" under his breath, and removed the dish to the sideboard.

"That's one poor ant will never regain the nest," said Eliza, smiling. "I say poor, but I must admit I have my doubts about the capacity for feeling of an ant. I see him marching onward, ever onward, round and round the peach, like a toy soldier, quite unmoved by emotion."

"And *my* feeling tells me that Latchett has put a stop to his march for ever. Tell me, are you interested in the customs of ants?" The tone was cool, but not unfriendly.

Blank faced, the butler once more offered the fruit dish to Eliza. She chose a peach, and placed it on her plate before she spoke.

"Jonathan, my brother, teaches me. These are wonderful peaches, sir," she continued. "So rosy, and so large!"

She had touched on a topic which held Mr. Darcy's interest; a slight smile touched his lips.

"We are proud of our peach trees at Pemberley," he said. "My father took great interest in his gardens."

He described briefly the way the peach trees were espaliered against the warm rosy brick of the enclosing walls of the orchard, and went on to talk of his succession houses, where pineapples and grapes were grown. "They need protection from frosts and wind."

He finished his coffee and put down his cup. "May I guess the name of my discerning companion?" he asked. "I think you must be Eliza Collins. I heard your brother discussing his work last night. He spoke well, and with enthusiasm. He wishes to travel, I understand, like the young man, Charles Darwin, he mentions so often?"

"I *am* Eliza Collins. And oh, yes. Jonathan wishes to see everything in the whole wide world. But most of all he loves the things that fly, and creep and even crawl. He collects caterpillars, spiders . . . My sisters hate his collections, and Mama has made a rule that he must keep them in a special room. But sometimes they escape ..." Eliza's mouth quirked into a tiny smile.

"And you do not dislike them?"

"No. It is so interesting! To see a caterpillar become a cocoon and then a butterfly! And Jonathan explains so carefully. He takes me with him to the fields and woods, when he is collecting."

It occurred to Mr. Darcy that it was a long time since he had known his own daughter express interest in anything other than adornment and entertainment of the more flamboyant kind. He worried, sometimes, for Juliet, who seemed to expect the world to accommodate itself to her. Her early prettiness, her winning ways, had made it easy to indulge her. He remembered explaining to his wife-to-be the faults of his own upbringing: taught what was right, but not taught to correct his temper, given good principles but left to follow them in pride and conceit. Had they made the same mistakes in raising their beautiful daughter?

Eliza finished peeling her peach, and sliced it carefully. The juice ran onto the plate, and she wiped her fingers on her napkin. The peach was delicious, her pleasure marred only by her anxiety not to dribble.

The butler poured a second cup of coffee for Mr. Darcy. He drank in silence, and Eliza kept her attention on the peach.

"I must go," said her host, rising and laying down his napkin. "Thank you for your company, Miss Collins. But tell me, do you always rise so early?"

Color rose to Eliza's cheeks, but her eyes looked at him with candor, and she spoke the truth.

"I am early, Sir, because I am going to ride with Henry," she said. "I long to explore the Park." Would he disapprove? Would he forbid them?

As she spoke the door opened, and Henry himself came into the room. He looked somewhat startled to see Eliza with his father.

"Good morning, Henry," said Mr. Darcy. He turned and bowed to Eliza. "A pleasure, Miss Collins," he said. "Henry is a fortunate young man.

Enjoy your ride."

The butler moved to open the door and Mr. Darcy left the room.

CHAPTER 9
OPENING STEPS

She stood several minutes before the picture in earnest contemplation ...

At present I will say nothing about it.

JANE AUSTEN

Juliet had promised to send her maid to help Eliza dress, but Eliza was not surprised when Agnes did not appear. She was somewhat dismayed, however, when, by seven o'clock, her mother also had failed to appear. Dinner was at eight. A quiet knock at her door as she struggled to fasten her bodice brought her eagerly forward, but the little maid who waited outside was nothing like Juliet's purse-mouthed Agnes. Instead, this small damsel dropped a curtsey and handed Eliza a bouquet of violets, "With Mr. 'enry's compliments, Miss. And Mr. Latchet said as if you thought as 'ow you might find me useful, I were to stay. I'm Becky, Miss."

Eliza buried her nose in the cool petals, inhaling their sweetness. Then she smiled at Becky. "Oh, please, could you fasten my dress? The hooks are so small and I can't quite manage myself."

Eliza's dress (quite the prettiest she had ever had) was white broiderie anglais, with a very full skirt, and a low cut neckline which had *not* been displayed before Mr. Collins. Her small waist was bound with a wide sash of violet-blue satin. The violets toned beautifully with the sash, but Eliza did not know how to fasten them. And her hair? How was she to dress her hair?

She was delighted when after a quick knock, her mother's voice at last came through the door. "Eliza, dear, it's Mama."

Charlotte came in quickly and set about her daughter's finishing touches. Her soft curls were brushed satin smooth, then curled round Charlotte's quick fingers. They were piled back and high, leaving one or two to fall around her face which, usually pale, was flushed with excitement. A matching violet-blue satin ribbon bound the curls into place and was fastened with a pearl pin.

"Now your necklet, Eliza, -- and where are your long gloves?" Becky came quickly forward with the gloves, her eyes big with shared enjoyment.

"And my violets, Mama? Can I wear them? Henry sent them -- oh, mother!"

"We will pin them just inside your bodice. There, that's quite perfect. See, my dear. You look a picture."

Eliza saw reflected in the long cheval mirror a small starry-eyed figure in crisp white, with touches of violet, her head topped with light-brown curls which shone like copper. She took a deep breath. But then she was distracted by the figure of her mother, dressed in black silk, standing behind her.

"Mama? I thought you were going to wear your new blue? You look so nice in blue."

Mr. Collins disapproved of color for married or older women. Charlotte's dresses ranged from pale gray to black, with an occasional mauve or pale blue dimity for morning wear. With the ball in mind she had begged his indulgence and ordered a dark blue gown which gave warmth to her face and gray eyes. But she was wearing black.

"It seemed more suitable, dear. And your father would approve. Now, don't worry about me. Listen, there's the gong."

They collected Jonathan, trim in his new evening dress, and then Charlotte led her family down the great staircase to the drawing room where the dinner guests were collecting.

There was considerable turmoil in Charlotte Collins' mind as she entered the beautiful room. Earlier, just as she was opening her door to go to Eliza, a footman had brought her word that a groom had arrived from Longbourn, with a letter from her housekeeper. The news it contained was startling. There had been barely time to change her dress, after reading it. Now the letter was tucked inside her bodice, and rustled faintly each time she moved. She longed to go somewhere quietly by herself, to think. But the time was not appropriate. She had made up her mind. At present she would say nothing about it. She had her children to think of. She sought distraction in her surroundings.

The first thing she noticed was the portrait of Elizabeth, by Thomas Lawrence, painted some ten years previously, occupying pride of place over the white marble mantelpiece. Charlotte knew that a more recent portrait of Mr. and Mrs. Darcy, accompanied by Mr. Darcy's pointer, Diogenes, was to be found in the library. It had been painted by Edwin Landseer. Mr. Landseer was not from choice a portrait painter; and had been coaxed into action by the inclusion of the dog.

Charlotte was aware that a portrait of Jane Bingley, painted recently by Sir Francis Grant, was part of an exhibition of portraits by Winterhalter (the young Queen's favorite), Lawrence and Grant presently on show in a gallery in Pall Mall, but Mr. Darcy had not wished Elizabeth's portrait to be displayed. "He is a little possessive," said Elizabeth, smiling, "where I am concerned." Charlotte thought the portrait brought her friend vividly to life. Elizabeth's head was high, and a smile hovered about her lips as if at any moment she would break into laughter. "Beautiful," she said to herself. "You are right," said a quiet voice at her shoulder. Charlotte had not realized she had spoken out loud. She turned quickly and found Mr. Darcy beside her, looking up at the picture with an expression of love and pride that touched her very much. "I am pleased to see you, Mrs. Collins," he went on. "I had the pleasure of your daughter's company at breakfast this morning. I congratulate you on her upbringing."

He moved away, and Charlotte stared after him. Eliza had said nothing of a breakfast meeting; she had been too full of her ride.

Dinner was a grand affair and Henry's duty kept him with the more important guests. Etiquette demanded that Lord and Lady Charles Baluster had first claim on the Darcys' attention. Eliza saw Henry sitting with his cousin, the Honorable Lucy Baluster. Henry looked serious.

Oh, dear Henry, thought Eliza, giving way to a sudden warmth of affection. Their morning ride had been wonderful. Such lovely horses. She had never ridden the equal of the spirited little mare Henry had brought for her. She recalled the smell of new-cut grass, still damp with dew, steaming under the early morning sun; the scent of honeysuckle warm in the hedgerows. They had ranged widely through the Pemberley park, jumped logs, raced down the rides in the plantation, followed dragonflies that led them on like will-o-the-wisps, and at last stopped and dismounted under the complicated branches of a great oak tree, old as the Darcy heritage. Sitting side by side on a log, they had laughed and talked and laughed again. They played "do you remember," recalling their first meeting, the cat and the caterpillar; they talked of poetry, which they both loved, and Henry confided his dreams of writing something worthy of publication one day. At last they rose to remount and, as Henry lifted Eliza back into the saddle, he smiled up at her and quoted:

> "*I met a Lady in the Meads,*
> *Full beautiful, a faery's child.*
> *Her hair was long, her foot was light ...*'"

"Oh, Henry," said Eliza. "And are my eyes wild?" (finishing the stanza). "*Not* a suitable quotation." And she laughed at him and rode away and returned to the house in a golden glow of emotion. Henry seemed to her just the same as he had been at Longbourn, quiet (beside his more boisterous brother), considerate and friendly, and with a look in his eyes when he turned to her that made her recite mentally, with some haste, all the cautions her mother had laid upon her.

The Collinses were seated towards the center of the long dining table, below the Balusters and Fitzwilliams, the Bingleys and Wentworths. Charlotte whispered to Jonathan the names of as many of the guests as she could identify, and he passed the information on to Eliza: that red-faced man with the noisy laugh was Sir Thomas Bertram; the beautiful dark-haired lady in sapphire blue was the wife of Colonel Brandon, who was the quiet man with iron gray hair seated next to Mrs. Bingley; the man in naval uniform, with his face weathered a deep brown, was Admiral Wentworth.

The meal seemed interminable to Eliza, too excited to take much interest in the excellent food. She picked at a slice of chicken breast, a mushroom fritter. Only when dessert was on the table did she reach out her hand quite eagerly to take a peach. She turned it in her hand. Somehow it seemed to restore the feeling of happy acceptance she had felt at breakfast with Mr. Darcy. As she held it, she had an odd prickly feeling of being watched. She looked up, and found Mr. Darcy's eyes on her from his seat at the end of the table. He looked down at the peach and up again, and smiled at her, and nodded. She smiled back. Then, contentedly, she ate it, together with some of the little macaroons of which she was fond.

But nine o'clock arrived at last.

CHAPTER 10
COTILLION

"Such very superior dancing is not often
seen. It is evident you belong to the first
circles."

"Every savage can dance."

JANE AUSTEN

The ball commenced with the cotillion.

This opening dance was arranged by Elizabeth
to be particularly for Juliet and Henry and the young
guests. Those of the older generation who wished to
dance would wait for the partnered dances which
followed. Juliet was to take her place at the head of
the first set but, when the time came, there was a
problem. All Juliet's plans had included the image of
Lieutenant Gerard Churchill leading her out; she had
kept two fingers over the first two dances on the
miniature program dangling from her wrist to save
them for him. But Gerard was still not present. He
had not been one of those invited to the dinner (his
parents were not close acquaintances of the Darcys),
but Juliet had been watching for him eagerly from the
moment the ladies rose to leave the gentlemen to their
port. Standing with her parents in the hall to
welcome their guests, who were arriving in a steady
stream, her face grew more and more discontented
when Gerard did not appear, and she was close to
pouting in her disappointment and chagrin, when her
mama summoned her to open the ball. The ballroom
was filling rapidly; the band of the Scots Guards,

engaged through Colonel Fitzwilliam's good offices, was playing a medley of tunes, and there was no reason to delay.

"My dear, who is your partner?" asked Elizabeth.

Juliet looked about her with a certain desperation. She, the belle of the Season, the one in whose honor this ball was given, had no partner! A tall young man with a rather solemn face came quickly forward. "Miss Darcy," he bowed low over her glove. "I should be honored." It was Colin Knightley, always punctilious in his manners. Juliet laid her hand on his sleeve. The band played a flourish. The dancers took their places in the sets, and the ball was in full swing.

Charlotte Collins led her son and daughter into the ballroom, her back straight and her head held erect as she had taught herself to stand when dealing with Lady Catherine -- her chin not high (that would have invited a put-down), and not low (the humble aroused the bully in her ladyship). Outwardly poised and calm, her mind in a turmoil, she looked around her and, finding a seat not far from Mr. and Mrs. Darcy and the Bingleys, settled her family. They were a little late arriving; the cotillion had begun. Eliza sat and watched the scene from her mother's side. Jonathan stood beside them.

The scene was a delight to the eye. In the cotillion, there was a swirl of full skirts, the young girls mostly in white or pastel shades which accented the black and white of their partners. Ringlets danced against flushed cheeks, and the light from the chandeliers, washed and polished until the cut-glass pendants shone like brilliants, made the smooth hair of braids and chignons gleam like satin.

Eliza saw Henry at once. She could not see his partner's face, but her auburn hair gleamed above her pale green gown. Catriona Fitzwilliam, Eliza recognized. How well he dances, thought Eliza, her feet beginning to tap under her long skirt. And there was Fitz, opposite Amabel. They seemed engrossed in each other -- her lovely face raised to his, and his look intent on her. And there was Juliet, exquisitely dressed in yellow, with a tall young man. They were not speaking. Juliet looked cross.

Elizabeth Darcy rose and began to move round the circumference of the ballroom, speaking a few words to each of her friends. She paused at Charlotte's side. She was wearing a rich ruby satin, with a deep décolletage, and a necklace of glittering diamonds. Her eyes shone with excitement -- as if she too were a young girl, thought Eliza. Eliza regretted again that her mother had chosen to wear black, instead of her new blue dress.

"Charlotte, my dear. How well you look, Eliza. A charming gown."

Charlotte congratulated Elizabeth on the brilliance of the scene. When her mother paused, Eliza felt she might speak. "Has something happened to upset Juliet, Cousin Elizabeth?" she asked.

"She has had a disappointment. A good friend of hers has not yet arrived. I think she hoped to open the ball with him -- she felt herself promised for the first two dances."

"With whom is she is dancing now?" asked Charlotte.

"One of the Knightley twins: Colin. He is rather quiet and earnest. As is his brother, Kit. But they are both very pleasant young men. I am so sorry their Mama could not be with us tonight. It is some time since I have seen Mrs. Knightley." Or her estimable husband, thought Elizabeth. Mr. Knightley was a favorite of hers.

But Juliet should not be making her discontent so plain. A lady does not display her feelings in that way. She is getting a little spoiled from too much attention. I must speak to her later.

The cotillion came to a close. The dancers were clapping their hands and laughing excitedly. The band master announced a waltz. Elizabeth looked around. She introduced Eliza to a young man in uniform, deeply tanned. Small lines at the sides of his eyes showed white until he laughed, when they crinkled into a brown mask. His name was Alexander Wentworth and he was a lieutenant in the Royal Navy, shortly returned from the West Indies. He made her a gallant bow, and whirled her into the waltz.

Jonathan Collins, leaving his mother deep in conversation with Jane Bingley, wandered round the ballroom, finding much to admire and wonder at. This was by far the grandest house he had visited. He walked casually but in fact had but one purpose. He was seeking Lucy Baluster. A group of dowagers caught his attention. They were seated in a half-moon of gold-painted chairs, gossiping and eyeing the dancers through their lorgnettes. He drew back as he recognized Miss Bingley among them. Her dress of black satin was cut low across a rather thin bosom and filled in with net, and her turban, of black and purple stripes and topped with nodding plumes and knots of lace, reached toward the ceiling. He had already identified Lord and Lady Charles Baluster talking with Mr. Darcy near the entrance to the ballroom. Lucy had not been with them. He looked about him and found, behind and to one side of the dowagers, an alcove partly hidden by a tall arrangement of delphiniums in a jade-colored Chinese vase, a stand of ferns and a marble statue of a Grecian goddess. Seated by herself in the alcove, pensively regarding her fan, was Lucy Baluster, becomingly dressed in white silk and lace. He came quietly to her side.

"Miss Baluster, I was hoping to find you. And hoping still more that you should not be engaged for the next dance."

She looked up at him with eyes suddenly alive, and gave him a quick shy smile, then looked down again at the fan on her lap. He made one or two remarks about the scene before them, but she did not speak, only smiled and looked away. He wondered if he had offended her in some way. As if to occupy her hands, she spread the fan wide and waved it slowly; it was exquisitely painted with a scene of butterflies. In trying to win a response from such a shy creature, Jonathan had already been reminded of his work with flying insects -- the need to stay still, then move quietly, so as not to alarm them. He regarded the decoration of her fan as a good omen. *She* was like a butterfly, he thought. One of the large, beautiful South American specimens.

"What a pretty fan," said Jonathan now. "May I see it, Miss Baluster?"

Faced with the specific request, Lucy's strict social training made her respond. She spread the fan wide, and automatically held it up to her face, so that her eyes shone over it. Jonathan blinked.

"Beautiful," he said, and the warmth in his voice and the look in his eyes at once melted her shyness -- and enhanced it. She blushed, but lowered the fan and looked fully at him.

"You know that I am a naturalist. Would it interest you to identify the butterflies on your fan?" he ventured. "They are taken from life, you know. May I tell you their names?"

"Why, yes," said Lucy, intrigued.

Jonathan leaned closer to her. "These are swallowtails, aren't they beautiful? And these are peacocks. Over here you have a red admiral, and three clouded blues," said Jonathan. "The small ones are tortoiseshells, and these are painted ladies. Is not that a charming name? They are very well drawn, quite true to life."

"The design is taken from a panel by Angelica Kauffman," said Lucy. She spoke more clearly. She looked at her fan with new interest. "How much you know! It is wonderful that you can tell me all their names! My mother gave me the fan specially for this dance. I have not been to many balls," she confided shyly. "You see, I am not yet out -- I haven't been presented. Next year, mother says. Little informal dances like the one last night are different. And this dance is for Juliet and Henry, so mother approved. But the noise and the crowd! And all the new guests

-- I don't know half of them. And people telling me all the time what to do -- and what not to do ... "

"Miss Bingley?" whispered Jonathan. Lucy gave him a quick glance, and laughed.

I wonder what Miss Bingley has said to her about me, thought Jonathan. A prohibition, so I imagine. The Honorable Lucy Baluster should not condescend to a mere Jonathan Collins. The band struck up again, and his ear was caught by the new dance just starting, a polka.

"Do you like the polka? If you are not engaged, may I have the honor of this dance?" asked Jonathan.

Lucy rose, shutting her fan, and took the arm he offered her. As they moved onto the floor, a strident voice behind them called "Lucy! Lucy, dear!" Jonathan moved quickly. "Don't look back," he warned, and Lucy laughed again. Soon they were twirling round the floor, at first a little stiffly. But it was hard to be stiff when dancing the polka. The exuberance of the music caught Lucy up in its excitement. She relaxed in Jonathan's arms, her eyes wide with the joy of the dance. Jonathan looked at her and held his breath. He thought she was the loveliest girl he had ever seen.

As soon as his duty dances were over, Henry Darcy sought out Eliza. They had not danced a partnered dance together previously, and found, with exquisite surprise, that their steps matched exactly. Dancing with Eliza was like dancing with thistledown, thought Henry. Poetic phrases formed in his mind. A sonnet, he thought. I won't "compare her to a summer's day" -- she is like a spring morning, a snowdrop, a dewdrop on a petal. He remembered a poem of Lord Byron's, and began to recite, his mouth close to her ear:

> *"There be none of Beauty's daughters*
> *With a magic like thee;*
> *And like music on the waters*
> *Is thy sweet voice to me."*

As the dance ended, they came to rest next to Catriona Fitzwilliam, who turned to smile at Henry before allowing her partner to lead her off the floor.

"Who is that?" asked Eliza, "The man partnering Miss Fitzwilliam?" He had glanced at her briefly and then away, his rather narrow but very keen eyes turning elsewhere almost at once, dismissing her, as if assured of her unimportance. He was a man perhaps in his thirties, older than most of the young Darcys' friends, his hair glinted with reddish highlights, and those narrow eyes were greenish-gray. A foxy man, thought Eliza. Her mind turned readily to natural history.

"That's Walter William Elliot. His father's Sir William Elliot, of Kellynch Hall. I wonder mother asked him; but Juliet saw something of him in town, I believe." Henry found Eliza a seat near her mother. He began to name other young people passing near them.

Walter William Elliot parted reluctantly from his vivacious and striking partner, but Catriona was claimed at once by the next man on her program. He moved to a quiet corner of the room and looked around him, savoring the moment. This was his first invitation to Pemberley, and he was impressed --

impressed with the size of the park, the excellence of the landscaping, the size of the house, the richness of the furnishings. Kellynch Hall, in comparison, was a gentleman's mansion; Pemberley was a nobleman's seat. He had taken advantage of his late arrival to explore the ground floor, the rooms set aside for sitting out (always useful to know), the library where cards were the order of the day, and the conservatory. Like a soldier, he always liked to be aware of the lie of the land. He approved of everything he saw very much, and he wanted to be part of it.

Walter's early years had been spent (with his step-sisters, the children of his mother's earlier marriage), in rented houses in London in neighborhoods that became increasingly select, as his parents moved away from the somewhat rackety style of their early association. They married (he was happy to know), before his birth, thus ensuring his legitimacy. In fact, it was the former Penelope Clay's pregnancy that had convinced William Elliot they should marry. He had found, somewhat to his surprise, that he enjoyed the idea of founding a dynasty, *his* line, separate and distinct from that of the then Sir Walter. Penelope, ever adaptable, had toned down her wardrobe and begun to court acquaintances who could further their social ambitions. Money was no problem; William grew steadily richer from investments overseas. First, they became respectable, and then socially desirable; assured, sophisticated, smooth-spoken, they began to be accepted into wellbred circles. William Elliot inherited Kellynch Hall when his son was ten. Walter enjoyed becoming the young master at Kellynch; he looked forward to the time he would inherit the Hall. But social climbing was in his blood. He knew he was regarded with a wary eye by matchmaking mothers of rank. His mother's reputation was not forgotten, only glossed over politely.

Pemberley was in a different league from Kellynch. He wanted very badly to be accepted by the Darcys. As the heir to Kellynch he had a certain standing, but his father, Sir William, now in his sixties, was a man of moderation, cautious, calculating. Not for him the extravagances and debts that had plagued the previous Sir Walter. Sir William's health was excellent; his tastes controlled. He should likely see a hale old age.

Walter was closer to his mother; they were alike in many ways though, physically, except for his fox-colored hair, he resembled his father. But he knew her well and saw her clearly, her insecurities, her need for reassurance, for flattery. He knew she had a taste for show which his father kept her from indulging too far. William Elliot held his wife on a close rein, remembering all too well his predecessor's downfall. Lady Elliot greatly enjoyed being 'Her Ladyship.' She loved Kellynch Hall, and did not tire of swanning through its elegant rooms. The death of Lady Russell, that staunch friend of the family of the late Sir Walter, had brought a younger, livelier family to the neighborhood. Their own fortune having been founded in trade, they had been only too delighted to dine at Kellynch, and hastened to return such hospitality. Other County families had followed their lead, time having dulled their memories of Lady

Elliot's doubtful background.   She was content.
Given her yearly trips to London or Bath in the
season, and an elegant sufficiency of gowns, she did
not rock the marriage boat.

Her older children, born of her marriage to
Mr. Clay, were both married respectably.   Walter
seldom saw them. His mother was fonder of him, he
knew, the child of her great success, than of them.
They carried memories of her early unsuccessful
marriage, of managing on too little money while
dealing with a husband who had a taste for gambling
and was too fond of wine. And, after his death, of
the confinement of the years back in her father's
house, seeking a way of escape, making herself
agreeable to Sir Walter and humoring Elizabeth
Elliot.   While Walter was still a boy, after they
moved to Kellynch, Penelope loved to dress up for
him. When William was away on one of his frequent
business trips to London, she would choose a ball
gown, adorn herself with such jewels as she had
coaxed from his father over the years, and teach her
son to dance along the picture gallery. Walter was
pleased now with his own agility; he danced very
well, and he spared a kind thought for his Mama. His
grace on the ballroom floor was one of the reasons
for his success.   His father was made of tougher
metal, but his parents dealt well together, he thought,
and he was fond of them both. But Walter William
Elliot was ambitious and quite as calculating as
Sir William, and he had no mind to marry beneath
him. Pemberley pleased him exceedingly. His mind
lingered on Juliet Darcy. A formal courtship would

not be permitted, but there were other ways.

A quizzical smile on his rather thin lips, he prowled the ballroom.

CHAPTER 11
FOX AMONG THE HENS

"Next to being married, a girl likes to be crossed in love a little now and then."

Their preference of each other was plain enough to make her a little uneasy . . .

JANE AUSTEN

At about 11 o'clock, there was a bustle at the entrance to the ballroom as some latecomers entered, with a certain amount of fuss and attention-drawing conversation. A young woman was making loud-voiced remarks on the size of the room. Many of the guests turned to see who could be attracting attention in this vulgar way. Juliet, dancing now with Alexander Wentworth, an old friend, lively and charming like his father, was smiling and chatting with the radiance expected of the belle of the ball. As the dance came to an end, she too turned to see who was entering the ballroom so late. She saw a young woman, with shining blonde hair piled high and ornamented with plumes, dressed in a sky blue dress in the height of fashion. The young woman moved with considerable self-assurance farther into the room, and her escort became visible. He was a tall young man in the uniform of a lieutenant of the Tenth Hussars, his scarlet coat, ornamented with lavish gold braid, slung over his shoulder. Juliet's cheeks paled. She did not recognize the young woman, but the man was Gerard Churchill.

Mr. Darcy had long since retired to the card room. Mrs. Darcy moved towards her new guests, and Juliet went quietly to her side.

"Mr. Churchill?" said Elizabeth. "Won't you introduce me to ....?"

Gerard bowed gracefully. "With pleasure, Mrs. Darcy, and with my deep apologies for our late arrival. May I present my betrothed, Miss Ferrars? Mrs. Darcy, Miss Selina Ferrars."

Ferrars. Elizabeth noted the pretty but somewhat sharp face, the arrogant tilt of the head with its massed blonde curls, the over-elaborate, over-bright blue satin dress, and the costly sapphire and diamond necklace around the slim throat. Quite unsuitable at her age, thought Elizabeth. Her socially-trained brain was running through its index. She knew Mr. Edward Ferrars and his quiet wife, Elinor, very slightly. They had quite a large family, she understood, but only a clergyman's income. Nell Ferrars was a guest that evening. Hadn't there been some family scandal? The younger brother, Robert Ferrars, had been left the entire family fortune and had run off with his brother's fiancée? This must be the daughter of that somewhat disreputable marriage, presumably extremely wealthy, hence the necklace.

"Delighted," said Elizabeth formally. Oh dear, she thought, catching sight of her daughter's face. Poor Juliet. Of course! What a tiresome young man Gerard is!

The music was starting again; it was the supper dance. Gerard led Selina Ferrars onto the floor. Juliet stood by her mother, her face now flushed with mortification. Gerard had smiled at her, his own

special crinkly smile, the smile he reserved for her --
and then walked past her to dance with Selina. She
felt as if an icicle had entered her heart.

"Do you wish to dance, Miss Darcy? May
I . . . ?" said a quiet voice in her ear. She looked
up, startled. The man by her side was not handsome
and of only medium height, but his clothes were
elegant and his address considerable.

"Mr. Elliot," said Juliet, as he bowed. How
could he expect her to dance? How could she even
move? She met Walter Elliot's experienced gaze and
her eyes fell. Could he possibly know what had
happened to her? That her heart was broken and her
life ended? Moving automatically, under the spell of
those greenish eyes, she gave him her hand and he
pressed it slightly as he swung her into the dance. It
was a polka-mazurka.

"I have stolen you away," he said. "I arrived
late and have not the good fortune to be on your
program."

The dance was promised to Charlie Musgrove,
Fitz Darcy's great friend. A moment before, Juliet
had been fighting the desire to scream, or burst into
tears and rush from the room. But she managed a
laugh. It was true; Mr. Musgrove would be so
provoked, and this was diverting. The icicle began to
melt, and she was able to move freely and even talk.
She began to feel a little daring, even a little fast.

"The polka comes to us from the Continent,
from Germany, Miss Darcy, where legends have
sprung up about the dance. To dance the polka, it is
said, men and women must have hearts that beat high
and strong. In fact, it is said that by the way you

dance the polka, one can tell how you will love!"
Mr. Elliot's voice was low and insinuating.
Whatever he said seemed to be somehow secret, for
her ears only.

Juliet blushed deeply. She looked up, her face
questioning, her eyes a little shocked. Mr. Elliot
smiled at her, his eyes quizzing her a little, and began
at once to talk of fashionable London, amusing tales
of people she had met, very slightly scandalous.
Juliet began to laugh. Her cheeks were still flushed,
but she had regained her poise; her back was straight
and her head high. Juliet's sophistication was only
skin deep; her ventures into society had been well
chaperoned. Her color came now from the slightly
risqué quality of Mr. Elliot's conversation and her
consciousness of his admiring looks and the nearness
of his form as he held her close to him and reversed
in the polka. He danced superbly. He was a
different generation from her brothers and her usual
escorts. His manner seemed a challenge she must rise
to. Her heart was still broken, but her breath came
quickly and the lace on her yellow silk bodice
fluttered.

Supper was announced. Juliet was glad to
have such a notable partner as she moved with the
dancers into the rooms set aside for this purpose. She
noticed Catriona's quick glance at him, and then at
her. Catriona Fitzwilliam was two years her senior,
and had numerous beaux in Town. Catriona sat down
next to Amabel Bingley, and Juliet moved
automatically in that direction, but her arm was
firmly held and she somehow found herself seated in
a quiet corner, cut off from her friends.

The supper was lavish and magnificently displayed. A whole peacock made the centerpiece, its tail in full display, and around it there were ducks in aspic and cold roast chickens on silver platters, a suckling pig with a crab-apple in its mouth, lobster patties, glazed veal pies, mushrooms stuffed with shrimp and cream, tureens of white soup, asparagus, pineapples and grapes from the conservatory, trifles, sorbets and small iced cakes of every description. Champagne flowed. There was a fruit cup for the ladies.

There were two long tables, with small round tables set about them. When most people were seated, there came an unexpected interruption. Fitz Darcy stood up, his champagne glass raised.

"I want all my friends to join with me in celebrating a great occasion. Amabel has consented to be my wife!" Everyone rose to drink to the happy couple. Mr. and Mrs. Bingley, and Mr. and Mrs. Darcy, whose consent had already been obtained, stood smiling in pleasure, and Mr. Bingley made a short, cheerful speech of congratulation. Amabel, radiant in her happiness, looked up at Fitz, and he looked down at her, and their affection was plain for all to see.

Walter Elliot filled a glass for Juliet, who looked shocked. She loved her brother and was fond of Amabel; everyone knew it was only a matter of time before they were betrothed, but she had planned that it should be her *own* engagement that was announced that night. Emotion and dancing had made her thirsty and she emptied her glass at once. Mr. Elliot refilled it. He rose and filled a plate for her with every delicacy. She nibbled a vol-au-vent and some asparagus and he bent his head close to her ear and talked entertainingly. He was drinking champagne, while she was drinking fruit cup, but sometimes it seemed that her glass was filled from some headier fountain. It was delicious. Golden bubbles filled her mouth and mounted to her brain. Her breath came more quickly and her laugh was more frequent. When she looked up, his eyes were on her, and this again was intoxicating. She found herself talking of Fitz and Amabel, and then moved naturally to Gerard, and the shock of *his* engagement. Miss Ferrars' overloud voice could sometimes be heard above the general hubbub of the room.

"He is a fool. Why think of him?" said her new admirer. "To forfeit you for a woman with the voice of a peacock, and the taste of a magpie. *They* are attracted by shiny objects and gaudy colors, you know. Forget him. He is unworthy of you. "

"If she is a magpie, what am I?" asked Juliet, daringly.

He looked around the room, at the portraits and tapestries and Chinese porcelain, the brilliance of the chandeliers, each with a hundred candles -- everything that made up Pemberley. To be part of this, to make Juliet Darcy his wife and have the entrée as of right to Pemberley, would suit him very well, he thought. He smiled down at her.

"You are an oriole, that golden songster, a diamond of the first water. You are like champagne -- you intoxicate me." His voice sank on his last words.

The excitement of the ball, the tension of her anticipation of Gerard, the shock of his betrayal, the heat, the light, the food, the drink, all were at work in Juliet. His voice sent a delicious *frisson* down her spine, into her finger tips, her ear lobes. His fingers brushed the back of her hand.

"I should like to take you away from this noisy over-heated crowd, to have you all to myself, for a moonlit drive through the woods and meadows, soothed by the midnight breeze. Will you come with me?"

Juliet trembled. Such a suggestion was far beyond a débutante's expectations. How daring it would be! But at that moment she caught sight of her mother's crimson dress, as she passed among her guests. "Oh -- I must not," she said. "I wish that I could. But I must not."

"Miss Juliet," an voice broke into their reverie. "Miss Juliet, I protest!" Charlie Musgrove, somewhat tousled about the head and flushed about the cheeks, stood before her, staring at Walter Elliot indignantly. "The supper dance -- your company -- was promised to me!"

"You were tardy, sir," said Walter Elliot suavely. "Miss Darcy waits on no man's pleasure. Your punishment was to lose your dance."

"Juliet?" Charlie held his ground. "The music is starting again. This next dance is also mine."

Walter Elliot raised Juliet to her feet, then turned her hand in his, and brushed his lips over her palm before he relinquished her hand.

"Later, my diamond," he said, and sauntered off through the crowd.

But he did not go far. Spreading his net, he began to talk to Mrs. Bingley; he knew how close the Darcys and Bingleys were. It would stand him in good stead to make Mrs. Bingley his friend. Then, somewhat daringly, he invited her to dance. Jane Bingley was delighted. She chaperoned her daughter to balls, but seldom danced herself these days. She demurred, but then consented. Her husband was in the card room, doing his duty, and she went willingly out onto the dance floor with this well-spoken man.

Then he danced again with Catriona Fitzwilliam. She had several seasons at her back and was far more sophisticated than her cousin Juliet, and had a lively sense of humor. She did not for a moment take his compliments seriously; he changed his tactics and soon had her laughing. As he danced, he kept his eyes open for Juliet, dancing first with Charlie Musgrove, and then with Torquil Fitzwilliam and Anthony Bingley.

Juliet was enjoying herself. She still felt the excitement, the heightened emotional state that her supper with Walter Elliot had aroused in her. Torquil Fitzwilliam was a match for her high spirits, but Anthony Bingley, pleasant-mannered and gentle like his father, and more like a brother to Juliet than an admirer, was taken somewhat aback at the way Juliet pressed against him in the polka, by her flushed face and brilliant eyes, and the flirtatious remarks she made. He was a little younger than Juliet. They had grown up together but he had never been one of her flirts. Earlier, he had danced with Nell Ferrars, and been impressed with her sweet and modest manner. Alice Bertram, daughter of the Reverend Edmund Bertram and his wife, Fanny, was also to his taste, with her air of fragility, though he had been alarmed at how soon she tired; at the end of a galop she had retired to her mother's side with her hand pressed against her bodice.

But Juliet swirled madly through the mazurka with her head thrown back, laughing in his face. In spite of himself, he reacted to her exuberance, and they spun together round the room. And thus it was that the accident happened. Unused to so much excitement, Anthony failed to observe how closely they were dancing to another couple, until they all collided. It was a minor fault; a bow and an apology were all that was called for. Unfortunately the couple with which they collided was Lt. Gerard Churchill and his affianced lady, Selina Ferrars. Miss Ferrars cried out in alarm, and then stood apart, the picture of affront, while Anthony and Gerard bowed. Juliet, not seeing at first the identity of the second couple, turned with a laughing face and eager speech towards them. Finding herself face to face with Gerard, the laugh died. She made a small, frozen inclination of her head to Miss Ferrars, which was not returned. "Gerard," said that lady, loudly. "These country manners are too much for me. Take me home!" She turned away, taking his arm, but managed as she did so to entangle her heel in the trailing skirt of Juliet's pale yellow silk gown. Juliet felt the tug and rip as stitches pulled loose at her waistline, and a tear showed in her hem.

The insult, to a Darcy, to a daughter of the house, to the first lady of the ball, was too great. Elizabeth and Charlotte, talking nearby, saw the incident and hurried forward. Giving her escort no time to speak, Selina Ferrars made a shallow curtsey to her hostess, said a few cold words, and swept herself and Gerard out of the ballroom. Gerard Churchill's face matched his scarlet coat. He knew he had outraged the Darcys. His gentle mother would be unhappy, and even his careless father would be furious at such an insult to an old friend. He had judged himself fortunate, at a time when luck was so confoundedly against him, to win the hand of a considerable heiress, but had not expected his betrothal to be conditional: Miss Ferrars had demanded that she accompany him to the Pemberley ball, of which he had unwisely spoken. Nor had he realized that her intentions were other than social climbing, but Selina Ferrars had had revenge in mind. Various snubs and put-downs from Juliet Darcy had long rankled. She knew full well of Gerard's flirtation with Miss Darcy. This had been, in fact, one of her reasons for singling him out, though his self-regard was too complete for him to realize that he was in fact the hunted, not the hunter. Miss Ferrars had wished to flaunt her capture, but she had not been able to resist a more overt insult, whatever the social consequences. Her upbringing, after all, had taught her that money was all-important in society.

Anthony Bingley, almost in tears at being involved in such an embarrassing incident, turned back to Juliet. But she was already being led from his side. Walter Elliot had taken her smoothly under his wing. Talking in a low tone, patting her hand, he led her off the floor. Anthony, left alone, turned a scarlet face to Elizabeth Darcy. "Aunt Elizabeth, I must a-a-pologize," he stammered. "I would not have had that happen for the world. Juliet . . .?"

"Juliet is in good hands," said her mother, hoping devoutly this was true. "Don't worry, Anthony. You are in no way to blame."

Juliet was vexed beyond words. She bit her lip and clung to Walter Elliot, crimson patches blotching her cheeks. "I hate her, I hate her," she said, when she could speak. "How dare she behave in that way to *me*?"

Walter Elliot murmured consolingly to her, in a voice pitched low. He led her to the punch table, and brought her a full glass he had poured himself.

"What can I do? What can I do to show them?" she kept saying. Only that morning she had dreamed of the ball, with herself as the center of attention, announcing her engagement to Gerard; he was indeed to be married but to someone else -- and such a someone.

"Do you really mean that? Then come with me, my beautiful, my golden darling. You shall be my treasure, the star of my life. Together we shall astonish all Society. I shall take you to my mother at Kellynch. Come with me. Trust me. From there we can arrange to be married."

"Yes, yes, I will. Oh, but my dress! I must find my maid. How shall we contrive?"

"Go upstairs, my darling. Your mother knows your dress is torn; she will expect you to retire. Then find yourself a cloak, take the few things you need overnight, and meet me at the conservatory door. I will slip down to the stables and tell my man to harness the horses -- then I shall meet you at that door." He looked at his gold hunter. "It is nearly one o'clock -- I will see you there in twenty minutes. Don't fail me, my darling." He pressed her hand, then lifted it to his lips, holding it there for a moment or two. As he walked away, she could still feel the warmth and softness of his mouth against her skin.

CHAPTER 12
ESCAPADE

"We had a beautiful night for our frisks . . ."

"You will laugh when you know where I am gone, and I cannot help laughing myself at your surprise tomorrow morning . . ."

JANE AUSTEN

Juliet stole down the corridor which led to her bedroom and quietly opened her door. She prayed that her maid Agnes would not be there, sitting in her dressing-room mending the strap of a chemise or a flounce. All the other ladies-maids, she knew, would be downstairs in and about the servants' quarters, where they would have a chance of seeing the dancing and the dresses, and would be kept supplied with wine, cakes and pasties. But Agnes held herself aloof from the other servants, feeling herself superior to all but Latchett and Mrs. Cleghorn, and Jeanne-Marie, maid to Mrs. Darcy -- and Jeanne-Marie was French, which meant, in Agnes's estimation, she didn't really count. So she might well have chosen to stay upstairs, in case her mistress ran back with a tale of a ripped lace or frill -- as in fact Juliet was doing.

But the room was quiet; everything was in order. For once, Agnes must have joined the other servants. Juliet felt an odd irrational spurt of anger -- for her dress *was* torn and in any other circumstances she *would* have needed help, and Agnes *should* have been there -- then shrugged her shoulders and gave a nervous giggle. She felt almost giddy with excitement. Now, she thought, what shall I need? Her heart was pounding and her face flushed. Selina Ferrars's remark was like poison still percolating under her skin. Insolent, hateful woman, she thought, her eyes filling once more with tears. Oh Gerard, Gerard!

But though Gerard had betrayed her, she had found herself another beau, far more sophisticated and charming than Gerard. Someone who admired and cherished her, recognized her as the star on his horizon, as was her due. Walter would take care of her and one day she would be Lady Elliot. Gerard was only a younger son. She found a large bandbox, and began to toss her toilet articles into it, hairbrush, lotion, then a nightgown and cap, rolled up and thrust in before she had time to think what they implied. Trust him, he had said.

Walter had promised to drive her straight to his Mama; there was no question of a vulgar elopement to Gretna Green. Trust him.

There was no time to change her dress. She would need another to change into -- and shoes. Oh, how difficult it was, she had never packed for herself before, never given a thought to such a task. And there was no time, and no room in the bandbox for a proper selection. She found a hooded cloak, and a close bonnet. She wrapped herself in the cloak, picked up the bandbox and, with the bonnet in her hand, tiptoed to the stairs that led down to a side passage, to the breakfast room and the conservatory.

* * *

Henry led Eliza from the ballroom.

They had enjoyed a delightful supper, sitting with Jonathan Collins and Lucy Baluster, Catriona Fitzwilliam and Alexander Wentworth. Alexander was droll -- he delighted them all with his tales of living conditions on board ship and his misadventures at sea -- and Catriona was merry. Her delighted laughter rippled out at Alexander's tales. Eliza felt sorry for Juliet, isolated with that foxy man on the other side of the supper room.

"Juliet should be with *us*," she said.

"Yes. I wish she were not so fond of Mr. Elliot's company," said Catriona, adding "He dances very well, but mother did not choose to ask him to my debut."

"He is a cousin of mine," put in Alexander Wentworth. "We speak, but we don't visit. I think his father once wanted to marry my Mama. But luckily Father won the day. I believe it made quite a stir."

"He is too old for Juliet." Catriona disapproved.

The subject changed and soon they were laughing again. Eliza felt as if she had been wafted on a magic carpet away from her humdrum world, into a land of excitement and splendor. The music started again, and the dancing. The touch of Henry's hand, as they danced, she thought, the warmth of his arm encircling her, the sound of the music binding them together, as they whirled and twirled as one person -- oh, life was glorious!

The music faded and ceased. Eliza stood, still in the enchanted circle of Henry's arm, her breath coming fast. The scent of the violets at her breast, crushed and warm, was intoxicating.

"Eliza, there is something I must ask you," said Henry. He looked around him. People were drifting off the dance floor, but the noise of talk and laughter was considerable. He held her hand a little desperately. Where could they be alone?

The conservatory -- the very place, he thought. Eliza, and jasmine and gardenias . . . "Come with me?" he asked, leading her toward the door, yet requesting, not demanding. Eliza's eyes were huge. She looked at him, and glanced up the ballroom to where her mother must be sitting, then back again at Henry. Then she smiled at him and left her hand in his and went with him out of the door and down the hall. The conservatory doors were open and the lanterns lit; it was always used for sitting out but at the moment seemed deserted. They did not see a tall dark figure in a far corner, looking out of a window. The heady perfume of the tropical flowers after the heat of the day was almost tangible, but there was another scent, Eliza thought. She sniffed. Was someone smoking a cheroot? Eliza breathed deeply, and felt dizzy with warmth and excitement and scent. Henry led her to a white-painted iron bench under a moonflower tree and she sat down, her eyes on his.

"Eliza, dear Eliza," he said, dropping to one knee. "Oh, Eliza, I don't know how to say this -- but I love you so very much. Will you -- *please* will you -- honor me with your hand in marriage?"

"Yes, Henry," said Eliza.

"Sweetest, funniest Eliza," said Henry, as he raised her small hand to his lips. She thought them the most beautiful words she had ever heard.

* * *

It was such a blissful moment that at first neither of them noticed an intruder, a cloaked figure struggling down the center pathway, pushing between the bushes, hampered by a bandbox and a bonnet. The intruder was trying to be quiet, but her bonnet strings caught in a passion-fruit vine and in trying to untangle them she dropped the bandbox. "Oh, oh, oh ..." said an agitated voice, a familiar voice.

Returning to earth, Eliza and Henry drew back and stared at the newcomer. "It's Juliet," whispered Eliza. "Wherever can she be going?"

Hand in hand, they moved after her. Juliet was so absorbed in her own activities that she did not see or hear them, and when Eliza touched her on her shoulder, she gave a small shriek, and dropped the bandbox once more. This time it came unfastened, and her nightgown uncurled itself on the mossy path before them all.

"Juliet!" said Henry. "What are you doing? Where are you going? Have you taken leave of your senses?"

"Oh, Henry, do be quiet! And go away. How tiresome you are! And Eliza. It is not your concern. You are not wanted! I know exactly what I am doing."

She opened the outside door of the conservatory and peered into the semi-darkness. In the distance a fox barked. An owl, ghostly in the moonlight, swooped across the lawn, barely veering to snatch up a moth which fluttered, white and silent, and was gone. Where was Walter? Why didn't he come? Henry was going to spoil everything.

Eliza had noticed Juliet on and off throughout the evening, looking so beautiful and so cross. And then, dancing with that -- that *fox*-man, the fox's bark nudging her imagination. Walter Elliot. Juliet had sat with him at supper, tucked away in a corner, as if they wanted to be private. Eliza was suddenly certain.

"Juliet, are you eloping? With Mr. Elliot?"

"N-no, of course not. Not eloping exactly. Oh, do go away. You are spoiling everything."

Eliza saw a movement in the shadows, across the lawn where the brick wall hid the peach orchard, and the path led to the stables. Someone was approaching.

"Juliet, you can't! Think what father would say. I won't let you." Henry spoke in a harsh whisper.

"What do I care what people will say? Go away, Henry. You are only a boy. What do you know about life? Don't you dare try to stop me." Juliet was whispering too, but her voice began to rise. She had been getting steadily more nervous since leaving her bedroom. The vines and branches of the conservatory seemed to impede her, to clutch at her, green fingers stretched out to hold her back. But Henry's opposition braced her determination.

Henry was only her brother. It was no concern of his what she did. And Eliza was a poor relation!

(In the far corner of the conservatory the tall male figure put out its cheroot and moved forward.)

The fox barked again.

Walter Elliot was plainly visible now, padding silently over the grass from the direction of the stables. Henry's hand was on Juliet's arm, but she tugged herself free. Her cloak was tossed back over her shoulders; a lock of dark hair, pulled loose by her battle with the vine, fell over her cheek. Her breast rose and fell, showing the deep décolletage of her dress.

As she pulled away from Henry toward the door, Eliza's hand shot out. From the corner of its web, she scooped up the ginger-spotted, fat-bodied spider she had admired the day before and, before it had finished uncurling its legs inside her palm, she dropped it into the bodice of Juliet's pale yellow gown.

Juliet screamed. Her bonnet went flying, she dropped her bandbox, and she leaped into the air, screaming and screaming and making flapping movements with her hands against her chest. Her face was scarlet. Her cloak slid from her shoulders.

Out in the garden, Walter Elliot stopped short. He was quite close and could plainly make out the identity of the lady in distress. What had happened, he had no idea. He could see that there were several people on the scene. It was the worst possible situation for the delicate task he had set himself. He turned on his heels, and strode off back towards the stables. It was a blow to his ambitions, but perhaps it would be best if he returned to town without delay.

* * *

Juliet was a strong and healthy young woman. When she screamed, she screamed. The band was between dances, and the screams were plainly to be heard.

Footmen came running, and guests arrived from the ballroom.

"What is it, what is it? What has happened? Is it a riot?" people called.

A crowd was collecting. Eliza nudged Henry. She picked up Juliet's bonnet and he reached for the cloak and bandbox. Together they retreated backwards through the growing crowd. Juliet still screamed and beat at her bodice.

"Juliet!" Mr. Darcy reached the group. He seldom raised his voice. On this occasion he did so. And Juliet was shocked into closing her mouth. She still panted. Elizabeth Darcy came hurrying from the far end of the ballroom, but it was Charlotte Collins who was the first adult woman to arrive.

"My dear," she said, taking Juliet in her calm and comforting arms. "Tell me what is the matter?"

Now somewhat under control, Juliet was able to examine the neckline of her dress. The spider, limp, half squashed, its legs faintly squirming, was revealed, plastered against her skin. Juliet let out a last agonized wail, and Charlotte deftly removed the spider from her dress and dropped it on the ground.

"It was a spider. The biggest thing! Oh, father, it jumped on me!" said Juliet. Despite her near hysteria, she had seen Walter Elliot's retreat.

She looked down hastily, and realized her cloak and bonnet were gone. So were Eliza and Henry. "I . . . I was so warm. I was just going outside for some air. And then the spider . . . oh, Father," said Juliet, and threw herself on her father's chest.

Calm was soon restored. As the story spread, a thrill of horror, followed by a flood of eagerly expressed sympathy, engulfed the feminine half of the dancers. Ravishment was forgotten; footpads dismissed. More and more young ladies exclaimed and fluttered their fans; more and more young gentlemen wished they had been there to assist Mr. Darcy's lovely daughter. Nothing depicted in *The Monk* or *Udolpho* could compare.

"In her bodice? Oh, horror! A wonder she did not run mad!"

"*I* should have fainted, I am quite sure!"

"Indeed, yes. Poor, poor Juliet!"

It was felt a thoroughly reasonable explanation. Only Elizabeth, joining her husband and her daughter, as they re-entered the ballroom, looked at him and then at Charlotte with her eyebrows raised.

Charlotte pressed Juliet's hand, and Mr. Darcy handed over his semi-restored daughter to the eager attentions of Colin Knightley. Juliet clung to Colin's arm in a manner very pleasing to him. He felt strong and protective. Excitement had taken its toll and his quiet voice and deferential manner were exactly what Juliet needed. Colin led her to the refreshment table and plied her with fruit cup. Juliet, still somewhat dizzy with the concentration of events, was yet able to notice that the cup tasted quite different from that urged upon her by Walter Elliot. She was spoiled, but not a fool when not ruled by her vanity. She began to understand that she had been artfully encouraged in a certain line of conduct. The cure had been drastic indeed, but the need had been dire. And there was a brighter side. Though in a rather different way than she had hoped, she was indeed ending the ball as a heroine.

Some fifteen minutes later, whirling demurely in Colin Knightley's arms, Juliet came face to face with Henry and Eliza. Her eyes met Eliza's, and she smiled. It was a small smile; when she thought of what Eliza had done, she still felt an icy finger stirring the hairs on the back of her neck. But she was beginning to be grateful. It was a new sensation for Juliet Darcy.

CHAPTER 13
CHARLOTTE

Charlotte herself was tolerably composed...

"I am not romantic you know. I never was. I ask only a comfortable home."

--JANE AUSTEN

Sitting by Elizabeth Darcy, Charlotte pulled from her reticule once more the note received from the hands of the Longbourn groom, though already she knew it by heart. Mrs. Spong, her house keeper, wrote in considerable dismay; her handwriting, used more often to inventory linen or jam, was difficult to decipher. But the content was only too plain. Mr. Collins was dead of a heart attack.

"I took him his supper," wrote Mrs. Spong in a hand that wobbled across the page. "Nothing inflammatory, nothing rich - just a poached sole with parsley sauce and a nice baked apple - he was so fond of a nice baked apple, with honey and a squeeze of lemon juice, the way Cook does them. He was reading earnestly. I put his tray down on the commode and coughed to attract his attention. He started, pulled his eyes from the page and looked up at me. 'Mrs. Spong,' he cried. 'Little Nell is dead!' And then he clutched his chest, gave a series of deep groans, doubled over -- and he died. Oh, Ma'am, I despatched Reuben at once for Mr. Merryweather, but there was nothing he could do."

Into Charlotte's mind came the picture of her husband as she had last seen him, sitting comfortably in bed, propped up by pillows. He had not seemed ill, once the pain in his foot was relieved. But he had seemed somewhat unlike himself. A little forlorn, perhaps? She remembered returning to his bedside to smooth his sheet and pat his hand, as if he were one of the children. Ah, well. Ah, well.

Charlotte had broken the news to Elizabeth at supper.

"I have not yet told the children. I want them to have this evening as a keepsake, a special memory for them both. I will tell them in the morning. And then we must leave as soon as possible, Elizabeth."

"Of course, my dear, everything shall be as you wish. But, oh, Charlotte!"

Charlotte felt deeply her wrongdoing both in keeping this shocking news from her children, and in not setting out at once for Longbourn, but she did not want to spoil this rare evening. It meant so much to Eliza, and perhaps (and this was a source of wonder) to Jonathan. I broke the rules once before, when I set out to catch Mr. Collins; I can do so now, in good cause. We act as we think we must, and have little idea of any but the short-term consequences, she thought, her marriage on her mind. But I should do it again.

There were no tears in her eyes. She had not wept for her husband's passing, and this she considered a failing. But she felt, she thought, not so much sorrow, but as if the ground had rolled out from under her. And her feet were still unsteady. But her children were foremost in her mind.

Charlotte had always done her duty by Mr. Collins. She had given him a comfortable, well-ordered home, such as he had never known. But she had also felt it part of her duty to balance his needs and wishes against those of her children. Always she had given him the respect she felt his due, as her husband and as a clergyman. Mr. Collins was not a man of intelligence or education; at best his temper might be said to be resentful or even sullen, but he was not abusive. He was easily jealous of the children, whose lives were so much happier than his own childhood had been, but he had never struck them, though beatings were commonplace enough in family life. And he *was* persuadable. Charlotte had learned how best to divert any harshness or injustice to the children that might arise; she cushioned the abrasion between man and child. One by one, she considered her children.

William had not been a problem. He was very much his father's son. When he was young, he had been something of a bully, but Charlotte had worked to keep that side of his nature in check. With his father's example before him, he always wished for the instant authority offered by the Church and the opportunity for public display vested in the pulpit. He attended a minor college at Oxford, as his father had done before him, kept the necessary terms, obtained a mediocre degree, was promptly ordained, and had been lucky enough to find a good living, at Highbury.

Mr. Collins saw no reason for Jonathan, who had no turn for the Church, to attend Cambridge as he wished. But Charlotte, recognizing Jonathan's lively intelligence and knowing it would be good for him to widen his acquaintance and meet men of a different stamp from his father, had fought for him, persuading the father that two college-educated sons would be something of which to boast. Jonathan had done well, and now had friends among many learned biologists, botanists and geologists, and would soon be working in London as secretary to a professor at the Royal Society.

The only problem with Catherine and Anne was to find them husbands. Mr. Collins thought all women should be married (he saw no purpose for them on earth other than as handmaidens to men. This, he said, was the will of the Lord), but he disliked the necessary preliminaries, finding the idea of courtship somewhat distasteful when applied to his own daughters, though he could not have explained why. Explanation was not in fact his strong suit; he preferred deferential, unquestioning acceptance of his pronouncements. But it was not too difficult for Charlotte to persuade him to allow them to attend assemblies and private dances with their Lucas cousins, and visit with new friends. Catherine was engaged to a very correct young man she had met while on holiday at Sanditon; Charlotte encouraged Anne, the less confident of the two, to accompany her sister when she could.

And then there was Eliza. Charlotte smiled to herself as she thought of this particular daughter. Eliza, holding Henry's hand, had come to her earlier to whisper of their engagement. Then Henry had departed to find his own mother and father. There would be no public declaration at this time, no intrusion on Fitz's and Amabel's glory, but it would come. Consent had been given. Henry was quietly determined, and his happiness was tangible. And since then Charlotte had spoken with the Darcys, and found them both accepting of this outcome. Mr. Darcy went as far as to say, unexpectedly, that he thought Eliza was a young lady of infinite resource who would be a refreshing addition to the Darcy family. A year's engagement was suggested, for Henry to find his feet, and this was acceptable to all.

What a triumph for Eliza to marry Henry Darcy. How Mr. Collins would have pranced! Charlotte felt a rueful compunction that he should have missed the chance, even as she thought how insufferable he would have made himself to Mr. Darcy. And for Eliza to marry for love, not just for advantage! "I have always had a taste for consequence," Charlotte admitted to herself. "It is a weakness," she thought. And she remembered advising Elizabeth, at the Netherfield ball all those years ago, not to be a simpleton and allow her liking for Mr. Wickham to make her appear unpleasant in the eyes of Mr. Darcy, a man of ten times his consequence. Her advice would not have changed. How right she had been although, she now admitted, perhaps for the wrong reasons. Elizabeth had fallen in love with Mr. Darcy and married him; her life was a success. Charlotte's heart was glad for her friend. She herself had never been in love, and her marriage of convenience had served her purpose. But Eliza, her precious Eliza, like Elizabeth before her, had a chance of achieving not just security, but great position and prosperity, with the lasting blessing of true affection.

Elizabeth was speaking to her again. She collected her thoughts.

"You must go tomorrow, of course. But why not leave the children here? Henry will not wish to part with Eliza so soon, and Jonathan has proved so good with Lucy Baluster (such a shy child). They could follow in a day or so, for the funeral."

Charlotte looked with gratitude at her friend. "That would indeed be acceptable, Elizabeth. It is somewhat remiss but there would be no *public* impropriety. William and Eugenia will have to travel from Highbury; my elder daughters are visiting at Sanditon. They must all be sent for, and it will be quite suitable if they all arrive about the same time."

They sat in silence for some moments, watching the dancers circle in front of them.

"Forgive me if I invade your privacy, but have you ever regretted your marriage?" asked Elizabeth.

Charlotte looked down at her hands, folded in her lap.

"No," she said, after a moment. "No. When I have been tempted to repine -- and oh, Elizabeth, I must confess there were times -- I have reminded myself of what my life should have been if I had never married. I think of poor Maria -- and remember that that would have been me -- and I know what I did was for the best." (Maria Lucas had not married, and now lived with her widowed mother in a small house financed by her brothers. Lady Lucas was in her late seventies, her wits were wandering and she was very difficult to manage. Maria was some nine years younger than Charlotte, but looked far older.)

Miss Bingley passed by at that moment, all nodding plumes like a carriage horse, parading with the Hon. Mrs. John Yates, in puce satin, and Lady Bertram, in an unfortunate olive green. Charlotte took note. That was the other alternative to Maria, she thought. If I had never married, I might have been like Caroline Bingley. Bitter and resentful. Miss Bingley at least had money of her own, but Society and her own conventionality had allowed her no house, and of course she had no children. Something tight and hard within Charlotte's bosom expanded and softened. Without thinking highly either of men or matrimony, as a young woman marriage had always been her object; it was the only honorable provision for well-educated young women of small fortune, however uncertain of giving happiness. She had not loved her husband, poor Mr. Collins, blighted from childhood, but she could be grateful to him. He had given her what she had wanted most in life.

"What will you do now?" asked Elizabeth, remembering her own mother's fears, and her determined incomprehension of the entail of Longbourn.

"For the moment, I do not see my way," said Charlotte. Her forehead was creased with worry but her hands stayed quietly in her lap. "William and his wife will move into Longbourn with all due speed, and I fear I cannot like Eugenia. I do not think we shall deal well together." William Collins's wife, the former Eugenia Elton, was a disagreeable young woman, snobbish and pretentious, with a sharp tongue.

"My dear, I wish to make a suggestion. I am sure Mr. Darcy will agree. Come to Pemberley and live in the Dower House. It is empty, since the death of Great-Aunt Ernestine, and needs a tenant to maintain its well-being. And if the time comes that I need it for myself (and I hope and pray Mr. Darcy and I expire together, and burst into heaven arm in arm), I am sure you and I will happily share it."

Charlotte found herself moved to tears. What her husband's death could not bring about, this unexpected kindness achieved. Her friendship with Elizabeth Bennet had been one of the rewards of her life. Charlotte had known Elizabeth since childhood -- the families had always been close -- but Charlotte was seven years older than Elizabeth and until Elizabeth reached fifteen, they had not been much together. Then they had begun to find pleasure in each other's company. Both were intelligent, thoughtful, fond of long walks and the observation of humanity in the form of their neighbors. The quiet, self-possessed Charlotte had watched with admiration the development of the younger girl, with her vivid face, amusing tongue, and love of life and laughter. She had always felt Elizabeth was bound for great things, a fine position, and so it had proved. The love and admiration Charlotte felt for Elizabeth Bennet was surpassed only by her admiration for Mrs. Darcy. And there had been more than passive admiration; there had been true friendship and enjoyment of each other's company, despite differences of opinion and judgment. Going away from Elizabeth had been one of the drawbacks to her marriage. Their steady correspondence, recording the small events of their daily lives, had been a compensation.

Sitting in the ballroom through the long and glittering evening, burdened by her secret, Charlotte had thought long and hard. Distracted briefly by the excitement of Juliet's escapade (and she had seen enough to know there was much untold on that score. Where, for instance, was the suave Mr. Elliot, so much to the fore earlier in the evening?), and then the joy of her best-loved daughter's engagement, the weight of her pondering had returned. What was she to do? Where was she to live? There was some money saved; she had always been a careful housekeeper, and had kept in mind her daughters' need for dowries. But she would not be allowed to live alone. Convention demanded that William and Eugenia offer her a home with them at Longbourn, but she could think of such an arrangement only with repugnance. Now this unexpected kindness from Elizabeth, on top of all else, was almost to much for her. She was used to bearing her burdens alone and silently. To be offered help -- and such help -- was overwhelming.

She blotted the moisture from her eyes surreptitiously, and straightened her spine. The Dower House. All her life Charlotte had loved houses. Living at home in her mother's shadow, as the years passed and her youth receded, she had longed for a free hand, the right to make decisions and arrange her rooms, order her servants, plan her days as she wished. She had won that right and, despite the presence of Mr. Collins and the interference of Lady Catherine de Bourgh, had enjoyed her home at Hunsford Parsonage (and Rosings, after all, detached from Lady Catherine, was a handsome building). Then had come the move to Longbourn, back to the neighborhood she knew and loved, and the house that had once sheltered her friend. With the greater elegance of the country house and the security of a comfortable income not dependent upon Lady Catherine's good will, Charlotte had been most content. She had never imagined anything more to her liking, and the thought of living at Longbourn under the patronage of Eugenia Elton was deeply dismaying.

To move to Pemberley, to live near Elizabeth and possibly Eliza and Henry (and without Mr. Collins), in the elegance of the Dower House, was as near to perfect happiness as she could wish. She had done her duty by the marriage bed, enduring Mr. Collins's sticky fumblings while planning her menus for the next day; now, to sleep alone would be a great comfort. What had she done, she wondered, to deserve such bounty?

Thinking back on the order of her life, she recalled the circumstances of her marriage, her unmaidenly behavior in taking it upon herself to seek out Mr. Collins and thrust herself before his eyes, her deliberate extraction (there was no other word) of a proposal from him. Where had the courage come from? At no other time in her young life had she so asserted herself. She had kept her composure in the face of Elizabeth's huge surprise and dismay, but she had felt her friend's disapproval strongly. Later, she had learned to deal with the intimacies of marriage, to command her feelings and make her own way, despite Lady Catherine's attempts at interference and her husband's toad-eating ways. Her child-bearing years had been difficult. She had badly missed Elizabeth; she had felt the need of a confidant, an understanding friend with whom to talk openly, as she struggled to carry out her household duties after her miscarriages. And then Eliza, so small, so frail at birth, and she herself not strong. But she was determined to rear the tiny child. And the two little boys, such little, little boys, who died -- and Mr. Collins, talking with his mouth full, saying they had gone to God and were better out of this sinful world, and then asking for a second helping of roast pork -- no, not all life was easy. There had been times of despair, of deep unhappiness. But Eliza had thriven, and Jonathan had grown to be her dear companion. And now here she was.

She sat back, tired but almost content as the long evening came to an end, and she watched the dancers. The consequences of her unconventional acquisition of a husband were there before her: Eliza dancing so happily in Henry Darcy's arms, and Jonathan, proud and tender, looking down at Lucy Baluster -- *that* was an unexpected happening. And there were Amabel Bingley and Fitzwilliam Darcy, Catriona Fitzwilliam with dashing Alexander Wentworth, Anthony Bingley with Nell Ferrars, lovely Dorothea Brandon with quiet Kit Knightley. Not all these pairings would come to anything, but it was a pleasure to see how these nice young people came together. Even Juliet, pretty, spoiled Juliet, seemed content and not unhappy, in the trustworthy arms of Colin Knightley.

Sitting next to Charlotte, Elizabeth Darcy too watched her children dance round the ballroom, then found her view was blocked. Her husband stood before her.

"My dear," said Mr. Darcy, extending his hand. "Will you waltz with me?"

Elizabeth held up her arms. They took to the floor, joining the throng, which fell back a little as they were recognized. The shimmering light from the candelabra was reflected on Elizabeth's elegant cheek-bones and the Darcy diamonds at her throat. Gravely and beautifully, Mr. and Mrs. Darcy waltzed round the floor.

"Dearest, loveliest Elizabeth," said Mr. Darcy to his wife of twenty-five years, and he drew her a little closer.

And Charlotte Collins, widow, watched with pleasure. Some things work out well, she thought. One must accept the consequences. She sighed a little, and closed her eyes. She was very tired. There was a great deal on her mind, but for the moment she could rest.

THE END

JANE AT WORK

*The fireplace
in Jane Austen's room
at Chawton
is narrow —
as wide as
two live coals,
no more.*

*Consider her
writing in that room
day after day
(hiding her work
when visitors came),
the damp cold
of the English winter
shivering round her
shoulders.*

*How stiff her fingers
must have grown,
gripping her pen,
yet the words
flowed smooth
and subtle, laced
with wit.*

*Did she wear
mittens —
or was she
so far removed
from then and there
that no
inclemency
could stay her
hand?*